D1624904

BOOK OF SHADOWS

ALSO FROM M. VERANO

Diary of a Haunting

Possession

DIARY OF A HAUNTING

BOOK OF SHADOWS

M. VERANO

SIMON PULSE

NEW YORK   LONDON   TORONTO   SYDNEY   NEW DELHI

This book is a work of fiction. Any references to historical events, real people, or real places are used fictitiously. Other names, characters, places, and events are products of the author's imagination, and any resemblance to actual events or places or persons, living or dead, is entirely coincidental.

SIMON PULSE

An imprint of Simon & Schuster Children's Publishing Division

1230 Avenue of the Americas, New York, New York 10020

First Simon Pulse hardcover edition September 2017

Text copyright © 2017 by Simon & Schuster, Inc.

Jacket photographs copyright © 2017 by WIN-Initiative/Neleman/Getty Images

Case photographs copyright © 2017 by Thinkstock

Line art copyright © 2017 by Five One Ltd.

Ink splatter art copyright © 2017 by Thinkstock

All rights reserved, including the right of reproduction in whole or in part in any form.

SIMON PULSE and colophon are registered trademarks of Simon & Schuster, Inc.

For information about special discounts for bulk purchases, please contact Simon & Schuster Special Sales at 1-866-506-1949 or business@simonandschuster.com.

The Simon & Schuster Speakers Bureau can bring authors to your live event.

For more information or to book an event contact the Simon & Schuster Speakers Bureau at 1-866-248-3049 or visit our website at www.simonspeakers.com.

Jacket designed by Regina Flath

Case designed by Sarah Creech

The text of this book was set in Berling Std.

Manufactured in the United States of America

2 4 6 8 10 9 7 5 3 1

This book has been cataloged with the Library of Congress.

ISBN 978-1-4814-9202-7 (hc)

ISBN 978-1-4814-9204-1 (eBook)

EDITOR'S NOTE

The young person known in these pages as "Melanie" or "Mel" sent this document to me as a plea for help during a time of great distress. She had recently encountered my earlier investigations into the supernatural (published under the titles *Diary of a Haunting* and Diary of a Haunting: *Possession*), and turned to me for my expertise in unusual situations such as her own.

At the time she contacted me, Mel was convinced that dark, demonic forces were hunting her and would not rest until they had taken both her life and her soul. She explained that she had put off acknowledging the reality of this issue for far too long, and in so doing, placed her friends, loved ones, and indeed her entire city in the greatest physical and spiritual peril.

The pages that follow consist mainly of her personal diary entries describing the events that led up to this horrifying realization. Also included are a few records of electronic conversations she had with her friends, who were equally involved in this traumatic experience. Other than that, I have chosen to edit this document as lightly as possible, removing only elements extraneous to the main narrative of occult and supernatural occurrences, which is presumably of greatest interest to the reader and student of paranormal phenomena.

Finally I have elected to intersperse certain pen and ink drawings Mel created over the course of this period. Though this may seem like an odd inclusion, I'm confident that my reasons for considering these last as significant evidence of occult activity will become obvious to the reader over the course of the narrative.

Montague Verano, PhD
Independent Investigator of Paranormal Phenomena
Moscow, Idaho

All identifying names, places, and images have been changed or removed to protect the anonymity of those involved.

MONDAY, SEPTEMBER 12, 4:15 P.M.

I just did a bad thing.

I want to talk about it but I also sort of want to keep it a secret, which is why I'm writing about it here. That's what diaries are for, right? To keep our darkest secrets safe.

It's ironic, since my wanting a diary is what started this whole thing off in the first place. I've never had one before—I'm not really much of a writer, except when school forces me. But Lara is always scribbling away in hers. She says it helps, whenever she's feeling frustrated or angry or upset, to write out her feelings instead of doing something stupid. God knows I've done plenty of dumb things in my life—stealing, destruction of property, mouthing off to teachers, getting into fights. But I'm trying to quit all that now, and I figured if having a diary helps Lara, it might work for me too.

So maybe it was a little counterproductive to go out and steal a diary, then.

I don't know exactly why I did it. It's been ages since I pocketed anything. I thought I was over that little hobby. I'd even set aside some cash to buy a blank journal to write in, and I went to the mall fully intending to purchase one. Like a normal person.

I spent an hour in the bookstore there, flipping through the ones they had, but I couldn't stand any of them. Lara's diary is made out of recycled paper and the cover is pressed bark, and there's a strap made from woven hemp twine that you can use to as a bookmark. It's so very perfectly Lara, and I wanted a journal that suited me just as well. Something with a little personality, but spare me the pale pink crap with kittens all over it, or inspirational sayings at the top of every page, or Bible verses. Ew.

Maybe it's not normal to want to copy your best friend in everything she does. But the thing is, Lara is truly a remarkable person. I used to think I was pretty badass, picking fights with people when they pissed me off. I never felt so powerful as when I was punching and kicking the hell out of some asshole who picked on me or called me a name. But then I met Lara and realized that she is ten times the badass I am.

Lara's a witch. Which seemed . . . a little *odd* to me at first, because I didn't believe in witches. I thought it was like saying you were a vampire or a werewolf. But real witches aren't like the ones you see in movies and cartoons—it's an actual religion. Lara has been a practicing Wiccan for a couple of years now, which is so incredibly brave. Especially since nearly everyone else in our school belongs to this one huge, ultraconservative church that hates gay people and premarital sex and alcohol and . . . well, fun. And when I say it's huge, I mean HUGE—with about twenty thousand members, most of whom show up every week. It's so big it's made the national list of "mega-churches," and that's how everyone refers to it around here. Though the members call it the "church," as if it's the only church that has ever existed, or ever will—the rest of us call it the "mega-church."

As far as the mega-church people are concerned, being a Wiccan puts Lara in league with the Devil himself. That's fine with me—I prefer Lara's Devil to their judgmental, hypocritical God. And I think I could do a lot worse than try to be more like her.

With that in mind, today I skipped the mall and went downtown to White Rabbit. It's Lara's favorite bookshop because it specializes in rare, esoteric volumes, and they have a really good section on magic and the occult. White Rabbit is one of the few places in town that actively resists what's been going on with the mega-church, and isn't afraid of pissing them off.

I don't know exactly what I was expecting to find there. It's not like they have a big selection of diaries or anything. It's a cramped little box of a storefront, and they don't have room for much, let alone a library of journals. But something pulled me there today, and I found myself in the occult section. I scanned the shelves, noticing books with the titles, *The History of Witchcraft and Demonology*, *The Lesser Key of Solomon*, *The Black Pullet*, *The Picatrix*, *The Discoverie of Witchcraft*, crowding the packed shelves.

Then my eye caught on this one book. Unlike the others, it didn't have a title on its spine. With a cracked, leather binding, it looked much older than its neighbors. Most were paperbacks from the eighties and nineties with lurid, colorful covers. But this one had gold embossing engraved into its matted, black leather. I took it down from the shelf, my eyes widening when I felt its cover—soft and unusually hairy, as if made from animal fur. Gold covered the pages' edges, shining a bit in the dimming candlelight flickering in the store. More gold in fine, wispy lines decorated the front and back covers in a frightening design. At first I thought it was an abstract pattern, but as I stared at it, I started to pick out shapes—twisty vines and wilting flowers, animals with human faces, and sneaky looking little monsters. It was hard to see them at all through the delicate tracery, but if you looked closely enough, you'd catch an eye staring out at you, or a gleaming golden fang. Each one was different, and incredibly detailed. Thinking there had to be a title somewhere, I turned the book over and over again, searched its spine and looked for words hidden between the unusual figures. But nothing.

I flipped it open but couldn't find a title inside, either. In fact, I couldn't find any words at all. There was nothing but blank pages, all the way through. Each page was so thin I could see my hand through it, but at the same time they were strong and firm, like it would actually be difficult to bend or crease one.

But no printing, no writing, not so much as a coffee stain anywhere in the book. Not even a tiny little mark by the manufacturer. It was the strangest thing to find squeezed in among all these regular books!

My first thought was, why would someone go to all this trouble to make a blank book? But then it hit me—of course! It was meant to be a diary. Like all those other blank books I've been looking at recently. It felt like fate—that I had walked into this specific store on this specific day, and gone to this specific shelf and found this beautiful book, right when I was in search of the perfect diary. Clearly I was destined to possess this book.

So the obvious next thing to do was to bring it up to the counter and buy it, right? And I swear, that's exactly what I was going to do. But then, before I even started moving in that direction, nerves overtook me. I realized a book this beautiful and old and carefully made would have to be really expensive. Probably way more than I had in my wallet, more even than I could get my hands on. Holding my breath, I flipped open the front cover, where all the other books in the shop had their prices penciled in by the owner in a neat, light hand. But there was nothing there. I checked every surface, inside and out, but of course I'd already noticed the book was completely blank. I couldn't find a price marked anywhere.

I should have asked about the price, but I didn't. I panicked. All of a sudden, a strange and terrible feeling washed over me: a tightness in my chest, a panicky flutter in my pulse. I thought, what if it's too much? I had to have this book at any cost, but there was no way I could afford it. I hadn't figured for spending any more than twenty bucks on a journal. If I had to, I could probably scrounge up more . . . do some chores around the neighborhood, borrow from friends, wheedle from my parents . . . But by the time I managed all that, what if I came back and the book was gone? What if someone else walked in five minutes from now and snatched it up? I thought about asking the man behind the counter to keep it for me, but that seemed risky too. What if that drew his attention to how precious this book is? What if he decided he could get more money selling it to some antiques collector? Or a museum, or a university library? I'm not sure what a library would want with a blank book, but I was suddenly consumed with the idea that this was the most precious object in the world, and anyone who saw it would instantly want it. I couldn't chance that.

So I took it.

And it was almost too easy. The White Rabbit doesn't exactly have high tech surveillance cameras everywhere. There was no metal strip on the book to set off any kind of alarm. From where I was standing between two tall bookcases, I was out of the owner's line of sight, and he was the only other person in the store.

The fact is, I've lifted in much more difficult situations than this. At one time in my life, I would have walked out with this book just to prove that I could—for the fun of it. But I've really been trying to put all that behind me. And I thought I did exactly that. So what happened? I can't justify it, but I couldn't resist. I shoved the thing into my bag, held my breath, and walked out the door.

It's strange, though—the whole thing made me feel more anxious than I ever have before. Normally I know how to look totally calm and innocent in these situations, but this time I had no chill at all. I had to physically restrain myself from breaking into a run. I kept a quick pace until I was at least halfway home, and then leaned against a wall long enough for my heart to stop racing, and pulled the book out to look at it in the daylight. If anything, it looked even more magnificent than it had in the dim light of the shop. I could see how bright the gold markings were, and how intricate the pattern. I felt a buzzing sort of glee to think that I owned this object, and I let out a wild laugh right there by the street. But as I slid the book back into my bag, that giddy feeling crossed with something else. Something darker—a cold, creeping sensation deep in my gut.

I don't know, maybe it was guilt over what I'd done, or fear about getting caught.

But I'm definitely not bringing it back. I love it too much. Even now, at home, I can't stop taking it out to stare at it and run my fingers along its surface.

MONDAY, SEPTEMBER 12, 4:30 P.M.

Oh right, I forgot to mention one other thing. The truly absurd part of this story is that, after all I went through to find and get this book, I'm not actually writing in it. I don't know why, exactly. I've wanted a beautiful diary to record my thoughts in for so long, and yet for some reason I'm typing my thoughts into a file on my laptop.

But it seemed . . . I don't know, inauspicious? To begin my new diary by writing about this kind of shitty thing I did to get it. I don't want to spoil it right away with anything negative.

As soon as I think of something good to write, I'll inaugurate it properly.

SUNDAY, SEPTEMBER 25, 12:14 P.M.

Almost two weeks have gone by now and I still haven't written in my new diary. I keep waiting for inspiration to strike, but every time I think I have something to say, I open the book up and feel so intimidated by those empty white pages with their gold borders.

It's like a mental block. I keep telling myself, if I can get past this nervousness and write *something*, then the rest will take care of itself. So I thought, what about my name? If I put that on the first page, it won't seem so overwhelming to add more.

But then, right as my pen was about to touch the page, I started worrying if I should be writing my name in the book at all. If this is going to be my diary, that means I'm going to put all my most private thoughts in it. What if someone found it by accident? Do I really want to make it so easy for them to connect it with my name? That seems like a bad idea.

When I first found the book, it felt so right and perfect for me, like it *belonged* with me. But now I think it must have been meant for someone else—someone with more impressive things to write in it. Maybe a world traveler, writing up their adventures? Or a poet, making notes for their great epic? I could do that, too, instead of using the book as a diary. Perhaps its purpose is bigger than that. I could try to fill it with something creative—short stories or song lyrics. I don't know. For some reason, that doesn't feel right either.

I'll keep waiting and hope the right idea comes to me. Until then, I'll record my thoughts here on my laptop.

TUESDAY, SEPTEMBER 27, 10:23 P.M.

Okay, I have an idea: tomorrow I'm going to bring the book to school with me. I always have more to say in school than when I'm at home, so that might help inspiration strike. I've been thinking, if it's not the book that prevents me from writing, maybe it's being in my boring old bedroom, where I never do anything but homework and sleep. At school, there's always plenty to think about and react to and get enraged over—mostly the stuck up Queen Bees who see nothing wrong with being rude to everyone who doesn't go to their stupid church.

They're obnoxious, but impossible to avoid. The whole social life of Middleton High School revolves around them, their parties, and their clubs. All the popular kids know one another from church, and they exclude anyone who isn't a member. They're all mean and judgmental, and if you don't go to their church, you might as well be a complete social pariah.

Of course, they'd never admit that. They'd probably say there are other reasons I'm a social pariah—like wearing black every day and dying my hair neon pink and electric blue, and listening to dark, angsty music instead of their insipid God-rock. I've been going to school with most of these kids since we were little, and they have always treated me and the others who aren't in the church like shit.

I figured out early that there were only two ways to deal with these people. You can suck up to them and flatter them and try to force yourself into their narrow definition of acceptable behavior. Or you can rebel, reject them, and embrace the role of the unrepentant misfit. With the second option, at least you mostly get left alone.

Since I do have some self-respect, that was what I chose. But unfortunately it only makes them leave me alone *most* of the time. That means on any given day, there will still be people shooting me dirty looks, whisperings and giggling, being openly rude, and worst of all, offering to pray for my immortal soul. Is it any wonder that hell sounds better than any heaven where I'd be surrounded by these patronizing little shits? And is it any wonder I've been known to smack the sanctimonious looks off their faces from time to time?

Luckily as I've grown older, I've come to realize I'm not the only person outside the mainstream. Now that I'm in high school, it's easier for me to spot the other outcasts and try to bond with them. That's how I became friends with Lara. If anything, Lara stands out even more in this school than I do. She was actually raised in the church all the popular kids belong to, so it made some pretty big waves when she left it two years ago to become a Wiccan. She started out reading fantasy novels in junior high—wizarding and magic and all that stuff. Seems innocent enough, but the mega-church people threw a fit. They said she was putting her soul in danger by reading about wizards and witches performing spells—that these books were tools of the Devil designed to draw her into the practice of black magic.

The irony is, up to that point, Lara had never heard of Wicca. It was everyone obsessing over the dangers of demonic influences that made her look into alternate religious paths. And when she finally came out as a witch, the mega-church people completely lost it. Hardly any actual schoolwork was done that semester, as everyone was caught up in constant meetings over whether she should be expelled or forced to go to some deprogramming camp. People were having candlelit vigils for Lara's *soul*. It was incredible.

Anyway, that's how we became best friends. Not right away, of course—I admired Lara from afar, but I was too intimidated to talk to someone so brave and at the center of such a massive scandal. Then one day a group of kids were picking on me about the way I look, and I lost control. I grabbed the one closest to me and started smacking her, punching, scratching, and biting until she was bloody. It was stupid—there were half a dozen of them, there was no way I could win the fight. But when that rage builds up in me, I don't think clearly. After a minute, a couple of the others jumped in and started to get the better of me. They had me on the ground—scratched up face, bloody lip. It would have been worse, but that's when Lara came by and told them to stop. And they did, right then and there. She didn't have to use her fists or call a teacher or even raise her voice.

I could throw all the punches in the world and never have

the power or authority she had that day. It's not exactly that people respect her, it's that they're scared of her—afraid she'll curse them or call upon the Devil himself to wreak his havoc on them.

Whatever the reason, they backed off. And Lara and I became as close as sisters. Then last year she started dating Caleb Gardner.

I shouldn't really complain. I've seen it happen plenty of times—a girl starts dating some boy and suddenly loses all interest in her former best friends. Lara isn't like that at all—in fact, I can tell that she has gone out of her way to make time for me and include me in her life. I do appreciate that, but the fact is, Caleb's a dick. He tries to play like he's an outcast, like us, but he's been popular his whole life, and has never had to fight or struggle for anything. All because his dad is the minister of the mega-church.

Yep—Caleb's dad is the one responsible for all this bullshit that's been inflicted on people like Lara and me. Fifteen years ago, Caleb's family moved to town and Reverend Gardner became the minister at the local Protestant church. He was wildly charismatic, and pretty soon he had the whole town eating out of his hand. Which meant his kid was treated like some kind of Golden Child. Spoiled rotten, because everyone wanted to use him to suck up to his dad.

So how did sweet, brave Lara wind up with this jerk? If you ask me, Caleb wanted to piss off his dad, and cause a big scandal—*the preacher's kid dating the girl who made the news for practicing witchcraft!* It definitely earned him attention. As for Lara . . . she must see something in him I don't. But she could probably find the good in anyone.

Anyway, I've gotten used to him. What choice do I have? If I want to keep my best friend, I have to put up with the guy she's seeing. But sometimes I can't help wishing it could go back to being only the two of us.

One good thing about it is that since Caleb started hanging out with us, people do leave us alone a bit more. Thanks to his dad, no one wants to mess with him. Which is useful. I really don't care if any of those assholes like me, but I'd rather have them not harass me all the time.

Wow, I didn't realize I had so much to say about all that. I should have been writing in the real diary all along! Oh well, too late now. Maybe tomorrow.

WEDNESDAY, SEPTEMBER 28, 3:35 P.M.

THAT FUCKING SHITHEAD! I HATE HIM. Fuck this. Writing my thoughts down isn't helping at all. And FUCK CALEB.

WEDNESDAY, SEPTEMBER 28, 4:02 P.M.

I am slightly calmer now. I mean, I'm still really pissed, but I don't think I'm in danger of punching anyone in the face.

Lara told me to try journaling whenever I get angry, so I'm giving it a shot. And maybe it's half working, because at least I didn't hit Caleb (which would have been really stupid—he's a lot bigger than I am). But I did throw a mug of coffee at the wall when I got home, and now I'm in trouble with my mom. You'd think maybe she'd give me some credit for not getting in another fight? But the universe is not that kind. She handed me a sponge and told me to clean up the mess, but I'm writing this instead. I'll clean it later.

I'm glad I didn't rip the book to shreds, at least. I almost did—I thought about it. Even after I threw the mug, I was still so furious. All I wanted was to wreck something else. And the first thing my hands reached for was the book. Thank God something stopped me—I would never have forgiven myself for destroying something so beautiful.

Of course, the book is what started this whole spree.

Let me go back to the beginning. I brought the book to school with me today, as I said I was going to. I kept hoping something would happen that would stir me to write something in it, or at least jot a few notes. But by the end of the day, I still hadn't cracked it open. So it was after school, and I was waiting on the front steps with Lara for Caleb to come to give us a ride to his friend Lucas's house. We've all been hanging out there a lot since the beginning of the year, so it's pretty much a daily thing that Caleb drives us all over.

While we were killing time together, Lara pulled out her journal and a pen and started scribbling away in it. And I thought, well—it's now or never.

So I pulled mine out along with a nice pen, and I opened the book and started flipping the pages, trying to think of what to write. That's when Lara noticed the book. And she asked if she could see it.

Normally I hand Lara anything she asks for without thinking twice about it, but I hesitated this time. It made me uncomfortable to pass the book to anyone else—like I'd be giving her access to some secret part of myself. Which is ridiculous! It's not like there's anything private in it—there's nothing in it at all. Reminding myself of this, I shook off my anxiety and handed it to her.

Once she got her hands on it, I think she fell in love with it almost as hard as I did. She couldn't stop talking about how gorgeous it was, and intricately made and decorated.

I told her how I picked it up to be my diary, but that I was having trouble taking the first step. And she said, "I don't think that's what this book wants to be." By then, Caleb and Lucas had shown up and were sort of listening to our conversation. Caleb laughed.

"Wants?" he said. "It's an inanimate object, Lara. How could it want to be anything?"

I rolled my eyes as Lara explained that all objects have energy and vitality. Lara and I may not have the same exact beliefs, but at least I'm not a jerk about it. Lara brushed him off, stating that everything in the universe emits energy at a certain vibration, and some vibrations go better together than others. And then Caleb grabbed the book out of her hands and started to do a puppet show with it. He flapped the covers and made it talk to me, like, "Hey, Mel. I don't want to be some lame teenage girl's diary. Pleeeeease don't make me!"

Okay, I have to admit it was pretty funny at the time. But Lara said, "Look, even if you don't believe that, look at that thing! It's clear that whoever made and designed it had something special in mind for it." Lucas said he thought it looked super creepy, and suggested the book wanted to be some serial killer's memoirs. "No, nothing like that—but maybe for artwork, or a family history . . . or maybe something like a grimoire," Lara said, taking the book from Caleb, her eyes glancing over the cover as she quickly handed it back to me.

I had no idea what a grimoire was, and neither did the boys (other than Lucas saying it sounded like the name of a metal band), so Lara explained that it's a Book of Shadows—like a recipe book of magic spells. Magicians and witches in the Middle Ages would use them to keep track of their magical experiments and all the knowledge they had accumulated—incantations, rituals, medicinal herbs, that kind of thing—and pass information down from one generation to the next.

It sounded fascinating to me, and Lucas seemed intrigued too, but Caleb couldn't stop being a jerk about it. He was making all these faces and sarcastic comments about the very idea of a Book of Shadows, as if it was the stupidest thing in the world. I don't know what got into him—he was being an even bigger asshole than usual, and to his own girlfriend, no less. Lara and I were trying to ignore him and continue our conversation. I told her how much I liked the idea, except I didn't know any spells to write in it. That's when Caleb says "I know a spell." He grabs the book out of my hands and—ugh, I still can't even think about what he did next without getting angry all over again. He pulled a black marker out of his bag, opened the book to the first page, and wrote *abracadabra* in it.

What the hell???

I screamed at him to stop and tried to grab the book back, but that made him more excited about his little game. He and Lucas started tossing it back and forth to each other, playing keep-away with it. I was terrified the whole time that they were going to tear it or drop it in a puddle and it would be ruined forever.

Finally I managed to grab the book from Lucas and I took off. I didn't even look back when Lara called after me, because I didn't want them to see how upset I was. I started walking, and I hardly even knew what I was doing until I was all the way back home.

I thought the walk would burn off my anger, but it didn't really.

The dumbest thing is, I'm still not writing in it because now

Caleb has ruined it. After all the time and thought I put into figuring out the exact right words to write in it, he comes along with a fucking permanent marker and writes whatever dumb shit he wants in it. He's such an asshole.

abracadabra

Lara: Hey, are you still mad? I'm worried about you. Please get in touch, k?

Melanie: I'm okay.

Melanie: I'm sorry I ran off like that.

Lara: I don't blame you. The boys were being jerks.

Melanie: Yes.

Lara: Caleb feels really bad about what happened.

Melanie: Oh yeah?

Lara: He didn't mean anything by it.

Melanie: Sure. Whatever.

Lara: Don't be mad, Mel.

Lara: Mel?

WEDNESDAY, SEPTEMBER 28, 7:39 P.M.

I just got off the phone with Caleb, of all people. He texts now and then to set up plans, but I don't think he's ever called before. I was so shocked when I heard my phone ring and saw his name light up.

Only for a second, though. Then I put two and two together and figured out Lara must have hounded him into it, forcing him to apologize to me. I suppose that should cheapen it a bit, but I was glad that she cared enough to bother. And that he cared enough to go along with it—even if it's more because he cares about her than about me. That's still worth something.

Anyway, he dutifully apologized for his jerkwad behavior with the book. I accepted and was going to let it go at that. I figured he'd want to get off the phone as quickly as possible. But once we started talking, he wound up having a lot to say, and it was a pretty interesting conversation. He started explaining why he can be kind of an asshole about people's faith and belief systems, even when he knows it's better to live and let live. I suppose I shouldn't be surprised that it all comes from his relationship with his dad.

I had always figured growing up with the minister of the mega-church as your father, must have been pretty surreal for Caleb. But I never knew any of the details. Turns out, it was even odder than I'd imagined. When Caleb was a kid in the early days of the church—and before it became "mega"—his dad pushed him into becoming a child preacher. I didn't even know such a thing existed, but after I hung up the phone I looked up some videos online. It's bizarre! These young kids, seven, eight, nine years old, dressed in little suits and standing in front of crowds, yelling about hellfire and brimstone and Christ and the Devil. Like a real charismatic preacher, but in miniature.

I do get the impression that the kids don't totally understand what they're saying—in the videos, it's pretty clear that they're repeating phrases that have been fed to them, while waving their arms and shouting in order to give the impression of passion. I think they mostly want to make their parents happy.

That's how Caleb described it, anyway. He told me that even as a kid, he thought of it as a game or a show, and he hardly gave a thought to God or any kind of religious sentiment while he was performing. He enjoyed feeding off the energy of the crowd, and he liked how proud it made his dad.

His dad thought he was on his way to becoming some great voice for the church. He must have been pretty shocked when Caleb walked away from the whole thing. But Caleb said as he grew older, he couldn't do it anymore. The hypocrisy started getting to him, and he realized his dad was exactly like him—more interested in the power of holding an audience in his thrall than actually bringing glory to God. Caleb started feeling like everyone involved in the mega-church was either cynical and self-serving or gullible and self-deluded, and he wanted no part of it.

I have to respect that, even if it does make him act like a jerk sometimes. It's interesting that he wound up with someone like Lara, instead of a total atheist . . . I guess there's a part of him that is still interested in religion and spirituality, but only if it comes from somewhere completely opposite to everything his father represents.

Anyway, I'm glad I have a better understanding now of where he's coming from.

WEDNESDAY, SEPTEMBER 28, 8:06 P.M.

You know, it's nice that Caleb apologized and everything, and I'm not one to hold a grudge. . . . Maybe I did overreact a bit, and I get that Caleb and Lucas don't know how important the book is to me. They were only screwing around the way people do.

But all the apologies in the world don't change the fact that my book still has Caleb's stupid writing in it and it's still pissing me off. And it's not like I can make them go out and buy me a new one!

Dammit. I feel like the whole thing has been ruined forever.

WEDNESDAY, SEPTEMBER 28, 8:30 P.M.

Okay, I really need to get a grip on myself before I completely freak out. Because I seriously feel like I'm starting to lose it.

Still sulky after my last entry, I finally figure. . . Look, there is an obvious solution, right? The book doesn't have to be ruined. It's only paper.

I had this idea that I could tear that one sheet out of the book, and it would be as good as new, right? Especially if I was really careful and ripped it out right at the binding. You'd never even know.

I sat down and started to fold the page carefully along the seam, so it would tear better. But before I could even do anything, I realized my heart was pounding and I could feel my palms start to sweat. I sat back for a second and thought about what I was about to do. Could I really remove a page from an object like this? It could be precious, it could be antique. I don't even know what this paper is made of. What if I was vandalizing some kind of important historical artifact?

But there was something else, too. It wasn't only fear of damaging something valuable that held me back. I had this powerful, inexplicable sense of something like *sympathy* for the book—as though tearing the book would be offensive to it, or cruel even. As if it would be angry with me, and maybe even try to hurt me back.

I know, I know, that's completely delusional. But I can't even bring myself to write in this thing—how am I supposed to deface it now? It feels wrong.

WEDNESDAY, SEPTEMBER 28, 8:53 P.M.

I just spent the last twenty minutes psyching myself up, and I think I'm ready to do it now. I realize I'm being melodramatic, letting myself get carried away by what Lara was saying earlier—how objects have energy and vibrations, and that the book "wants" this or that . . . I need to remember that Lara probably meant it as a metaphor. It's idiotic to act like a book actually has feelings or can experience pain. It's nothing but a damn page!

And though it may not be the best idea to damage something so old and valuable, it has to be better than leaving it with Caleb's stupid scrawl in it. I can't bear it. So! I have an X-Acto knife I took from my dad's desk, which means I can at least do this right. I'm not tearing it up, I'm carefully and respectfully removing one page. It's like . . . surgery.

Okay, here it goes.

WEDNESDAY, SEPTEMBER 28, 9:03 P.M.

I did it! *Deep Breath*

I pulled myself together and cut out the page and it was fine—nothing out of the ordinary happened. I have to stop letting myself get worked up over such little things all the time. It's getting to be a little much. The thing is only a book, you can remove pages from books, it's not a big deal. And now I don't have to deal with Caleb's asshole writing anymore!

It wasn't even that bad. I sat down and slowly sliced out the page, being careful not to bust the binding. I was terrified that if I screwed it up, all the other pages would fall out too. But the binding held fast and I slipped the page out. It felt really good to crumple it up and throw it in the wastepaper basket.

Wait . . . Oh shit, what is this? There's blood all over my hands and keyboard. Gross.

WEDNESDAY, SEPTEMBER 28, 9:24 P.M.

That was bizarre. There was a LOT of blood, and it seemed to come out of nowhere. But I see now that there's blood all over the crumpled up page in the trash too—how did I not notice that before? I could have sworn that other than Caleb's silly scrawl, it was a clean blank page when I tossed it in there. And now when I look at it, it's seeping blood everywhere. Where the hell did all that blood come from?

When I spotted the blood on my finger, I figured I must have given myself a paper cut. so I went to the bathroom to get disinfectant. But the really strange thing is, after I washed up I still couldn't find a cut anywhere. I checked my hands over and over but there was nothing.

I don't know. Now that I'm writing it down, it all seems a little silly. It was probably a really small but deep cut that bled a lot and then sealed itself up so well I couldn't find it. Right? That obviously makes the most sense.

But I can't help it. Something about it still doesn't feel right—something I didn't mention before because it seemed idiotic. When I was slicing the page out of the book, I was overcome by this awful feeling. . . . I don't know how to describe it. It was kind of like the feeling I had once when I put disinfectant on my baby cousin after he scraped up his knee. He screamed bloody murder at the sudden stinging, and I winced from the knowledge that I had caused him pain.

There was no screaming this time, but the feeling was the same: that horrible sensation of causing pain to another living creature. Even without the sound, there was this awareness of suffering that seemed to slice through the air somehow.

I'm getting carried away with Lara's nonsense, aren't I? It's a damn book, it doesn't have feelings. I must be projecting my own issues of guilt and possessiveness onto it. Still . . . look at that page! How could all that blood have come from me without leaving any trace?

Lara: Hey, Mel. Did you talk to Caleb?

Melanie: Gee, how did you know about that? I don't suppose you had anything to do with him calling me. ;)

Lara: Mmmmaybe. I'm sorry! But I know that if you guys talked more, you'd get along better.

Melanie: It's okay. You were right, actually. I'm glad he called. I was mad but . . . I'm over it, pretty much.

Lara: Good. So everything's cool?

Melanie: Yeah . . . sort of.

Lara: Sort of? What's up?

Melanie: It's this book, really. It's getting under my skin somehow.

Lara: What do you mean?

Melanie: I tore a page out of it tonight. The page Caleb wrote on. I thought it would make me feel better, but I feel like I've hurt it or disappointed it. I don't know. That's pretty abnormal, isn't it?

Lara: Not at all! Hon, I totally get it. Objects can take on some heavy emotional resonances. Since it was second hand, maybe you're picking up on something left behind by the previous owner.

Melanie: Like how?

Lara: A psychic imprint, probably. It happens all the time. Objects always carry the energy of the people who owned them, and whatever was done to them. Maybe you should do something to cleanse its energy and make sure it's set on a positive path.

Melanie: Uh . . . that's not exactly my area of expertise. What would I have to do?

Lara: Don't worry, leave it to me. Bring it to Lucas's after school tomorrow and I'll do something. It will make you feel better, I swear.

THURSDAY, SEPTEMBER 29, 5:30 P.M.

Lara talked me into going back to Lucas's place after school today, even though yesterday I was swearing I'd never hang out with all of them again. No point in holding a grudge—anyway, hanging out at Lucas's is usually pretty fun. His parents are way more chill than most, especially given that they go to that crazy mega-church.

Or . . . you know, I don't think they go much anymore, though they're still technically members. Lucas's family joined the mega-church when they first moved to town—that's how he and Caleb became friends. Caleb's dad basically forced Caleb to hang out with Lucas because Lucas is black, and the mega-church was desperate to recruit more "diverse" members. It was this whole political thing—the mega-church's biggest competition in this town is a traditionally black Protestant church. Even as all the other little Protestant and evangelical churches around here shut down as their members flocked to the mega-church, the black church has always been a solid part of the community, and it held firm.

Reverend Gardner's plan backfired pretty bad because Lucas was the one who introduced Caleb to all the video games, movies, and music the church had banned, helping him see how much he was missing. And eventually even Lucas's parents realized they were being used—there's only so many times you can appear in the church pamphlets before it starts to look fishy.

All of which means Lucas's parents are relatively laid back in the parental supervision department. Most of the mega-church parents keep their kids so busy with youth group activities that they don't have any time for a social life. But Lucas has the whole basement to himself. It's nothing fancy: a stained couch, an old easy chair that had once belonged to his grandmother, a couple of rickety folding chairs, some crates we use as coffee tables, and a big TV that Lucas claimed when his parents upgraded. It has a couple of busted pixels and the sound's not great, but it all beats hanging out at the mall, getting harassed by rent-a-cops every twenty minutes for not buying anything. Maybe the best thing about it is it has its own door to the outside, so any of us can come and go whenever, without unnecessarily alerting the parents to what we're doing.

Anyway, Lara had promised me she was going to do some kind of "cleansing ritual" over my book to help me feel better about what the boys did to it. It's not that I really believe Lara has magical powers, but it was a nice gesture. And even though Lara's powers aren't real, I figure her cleansing could still have some psychological effect on me—help me feel like the book is really mine and that I have the right to put my own mark in it. At the very least, it would be interesting to see an example of the rituals she does as part of her Wiccan practice.

At first all she did was sit there on the couch beside me with her head bowed, completely silent and still. It was a little awkward for me—I didn't know if she was praying or if I was supposed to do anything, too. In the meantime the boys were playing a video game nearby, which was *kind of* distracting. But it didn't seem to bother Lara. She told me afterward that it wasn't a prayer exactly—more like meditation. She was trying to focus her thoughts and get in the right frame of mind for the ritual.

After a minute or so of that, she pulled out a collection of green herbs. "Sage," she said. "It's supposed to have cleansing properties." She held a lighter to it until it started burning and smoking. The smoke swirled around us, and though it made me cough a little, the smoke had a sweet, grassy smell. With a good plume of smoke going, Lara picked the book up and passed it through the smoke three times. "This helps purify it," she explained. Then she recited some sort of spell three times—I don't remember the exact words, but it was something like, "Spirits of nature, cleanse this object of negative energies and bring blessings of light upon it."

She put the book back down and looked over at me expectantly. I thought she was waiting for me to do something, but it turned out that was the end of the ceremony. Oh, except then she remembered that there was another thing she was supposed to say at the end: "So mote it be." Apparently you always say that at the end of a spell or a ritual in Wicca.

Then it was over. I don't know what I was expecting exactly, but the whole thing did feel a little anticlimactic. Still, I was curious. I asked Lara if there was something special or magical about the words themselves, and if so, why? They seemed pretty ordinary to me. I figured they'd at least be in a different language. Lara explained that it's not the words themselves that matter so much. It's more about having something to repeat or chant that helps you focus your psychic energy. She said that while she was chanting, she visualized a beautiful golden-white light washing over the book and purifying it.

I can understand why that feels meaningful to her. And maybe it even had some effect on me. I have to admit, I *did* feel better about the book when I picked it up and thumbed through it after her ritual. It seemed, warmer somehow. Not literally, but more welcoming, like a house with all the lights on and a good smell drifting from the kitchen.

I was so focused on these new feelings (or "energy") that I didn't notice the boys had quit their video game—not until Lucas was like, "So go ahead. Write something in the book."

I think he was trying to be supportive and make up for his behavior yesterday, but I wish he hadn't pressured me. I had been starting to feel comfortable with the idea, but somehow his putting me on the spot made me anxious again. And I realized I still had nothing to say. So I tried to hedge a bit, but Lucas said, "If you don't write something now, you never will. You have to break the pattern." I could see his point. But all the pressure kept making me more nervous.

"How about I start you off?" Lara interrupted, noticing my anxiety. She took one of my nice pens and wrote *Blessed be* on the first page in her fancy, curlicued handwriting. I didn't really know what that meant, but she explained it's like a Wiccan greeting—their equivalent of Peace Be with You. That did seem like a nice, positive message to start with.

But Lucas wasn't satisfied. He said if the book was supposed to be a Book of Shadows, shouldn't it at least have a spell in it? Lara looked over at me to check in, but I couldn't think of any objection. A magic spell *did* seem more appropriate than anything I'd be likely to come up with. So I gave her a nod and she wrote a little more—a good luck spell she'd used a few times in the past. Nothing fancy or complicated, but it was nice. It felt like the right thing.

Of course, this means that *I* still haven't written anything in the book—only Lara. But I'm not the one who knows magic spells off the top of my head. Oh well, I'm sure my time to write something will come soon enough. I do at least feel better about the book now. Maybe there was a good reason why I couldn't bring myself to write in it before, and it wasn't me being shy or neurotic. Because it's like Caleb said that first day. The book was never meant to be some silly diary. Using it as a Book of Shadows feels so much more right.

I have no idea how I'm going to fill it up, though. Where am I going to get any more spells? Maybe I'll have to go all the way and become a Wiccan like Lara.

Blessed be

I was a kid. At first I couldn't even figure out what I was so excited about, and then I remembered we had finally broken the block on my book and written something in it that felt *right*. And now that the spell was in there, it suddenly seemed that the most obvious next step should be to *do* the spell. But I didn't exactly know how to proceed, so I found Lara at school and told her I thought we should do it. She was excited about the idea—I think she was happy that her Wicca was finally rubbing off on me, and maybe she wouldn't be the only witch at school anymore. We agreed to perform the spell after school at Lucas's.

But first, Lara asked to see the book so she could make sure she didn't forget any necessary supplies when she wrote the spell. When she flipped it open to the page with the spell on it, she shot me the strangest look.

"Did you mess with this?" she quickly asked. Her question seemed odd—why would I have messed with it? And besides, it was all in her handwriting. Obviously it's what she wrote in the book yesterday. What else could it be? But Lara said there was something different about the spell. Something she didn't remember writing last time.

It turned out to be one word: *withershins*. "It's an old-fashioned word for 'counterclockwise'. I've seen it before in some of my witchcraft books, but I'm sure it's not part of this spell," she explained. I couldn't figure out why she was making such a big deal out of this. "What difference does it make which direction we walk around the circle?" I asked her. Lara said it didn't matter, really, except that a long time ago some people used to say that walking counterclockwise was only for black magic, and proof that you were in league with the Devil. But that it was nothing but an old superstition.

I think what bothered her most was that she couldn't remember writing it. I tried to reassure her, explaining that those kinds of things happen to me all the time. I told her about how sometimes my mind will wander when I'm taking notes in class, and when I look down, the page is covered in nonsense. Or if I'm trying to write one thing while people are talking to me or I'm watching TV, sometimes I'll realize I'd incorporated part of their conversation into my writing without even realizing it. It can be pretty spooky. Eventually Lara agreed that a similar experience must have happened to her—that she was writing the spell down while Caleb and Lucas were telling jokes, and some mental wires crossed, causing her to write something random from her memory.

We all piled into Caleb's car after school and Lara started gushing to the boys about what we were going to do. Lucas was happy enough to play along for the fun of it, but it was Caleb's reaction that surprised me. He went all quiet for a moment, and when he did speak, he said he didn't think we should do a magic spell. Caleb, of all people! He certainly didn't mind when he was writing joke spells in *my* book, but now that we want to do something legit, he gets cold feet.

I wonder if being raised in the mega-church had more of an effect on him than he wants to admit. He likes to present himself as this big atheist who has seen through all the church's nonsense. But if I didn't know better, I'd almost think he was nervous about the whole idea of performing a spell.

Lucas started teasing him, pointing out that Caleb has spent years professing his skepticism of everything supernatural. "What's the harm if none of it is real?" he added. Caleb didn't answer, and he didn't voice any more objections, either. He shifted uneasily, clearly uncomfortable with our plans. I suppose old habits die hard.

Once we arrived at Lucas's, we remembered we needed candles for the ritual. Lara has all kinds of different colored candles for doing spells at home, but she had nothing with her. We didn't want to put it off to another day, though, so we hunted around Lucas's house until we found some birthday candles and this vanilla-scented pillar candle his mom uses as an air freshener.

Lara said it would be fine, but I have to admit, it did wreck the mood a little. Marching around the circle with tiny birthday candles in our hands, the occasion didn't quite feel as solemn as it should have. Lara really wanted us to take it seriously, but it was hard with Lucas making sarcastic comments and giggling every few minutes, which kind of infected the rest of us. Even Lara broke a couple of times and we had to stop in order to calm down and "re-center" ourselves so the energy was right.

Finally Lara led us in chanting and focusing, and for a while it all seemed silly, like a kid's game. Then something changed, like gears slotting into place. I think I understand now what Lara meant about energy shifts. The air in the room all at once took on an electric charge. It was almost like a buzzing sound, only I couldn't hear it. It was more like I could *feel* it, as if I were receiving a thousand static shocks all at once. I don't think I was the only one who noticed it, either. Even the boys became quieter, more serious, more intense. It was probably all psychological, but it really felt as if we were doing something in that little room. Changing the vibrations of the space.

And in light of all that energy, I can't help wondering now if it's really real and we *did* do something with that spell. I tend to think no. . . . I don't pretend to have answers to the big questions, like what happens after we die, or if there's a higher power running this whole show, and if so, what it looks like or wants, but when it comes to supernatural events here on Earth? Miracles, magic, ghosts, ESP . . . I don't buy it. If any of it were real, wouldn't there already be a ton more evidence? Hard evidence, not some hokey websites full of obviously faked photos and stories? But I'd never say that to Lara. She takes her faith pretty seriously. Though sometimes I wonder if even she really believes it, or if she's simply very good at playing pretend.

Still . . . there's a part of me that can't help wondering . . . the same part of me that's all zinging and tingling with energy. What happened in that basement? What *was* all that energy? It felt so real in the moment, and I can still sense it pumping through me when I close my eyes and focus. There was something else, too. Almost like . . . I don't know, some kind of presence in the room. Like someone was there with us, watching over and guiding us. I know that sounds kind of sappy—a sentimental thing people say when their grandparents die. But I remember when my grandmother died, and I never felt anything like this.

I wonder if the others experienced the same thing, or if they're going to turn it into a big joke on Monday.

MONDAY, OCTOBER 3, 4:30 P.M.

I can definitely say now that it wasn't only me having all those feelings during the ritual on Friday. The minute I saw Lucas and Caleb down the hall in school this morning . . . I don't know, it was almost like I could *see* the afterglow radiating off them. I don't mean literally, like some visible purple and orange aura. It was the way they were talking to each other and their body language. Somehow I knew they were talking about what happened last week. I *had* to go over to talk to them about it. Normally I think of them as more Lara's friends and would be too shy to approach them by myself, but not this time.

Lucas was really excited about what he felt during the ritual, but Caleb seemed like he was working hard not to get carried away with the experience. He admitted that he had definitely felt something, but he pointed out that he's seen this kind of thing before. At his dad's church, people are always getting "overcome by the spirit," to the point where they tremble or shout or fall on the floor. What they call "the spirit" is what we're calling "energy," but it's basically the same thing. And just because it *feels* powerful doesn't mean there's anything supernatural about it. It's nothing but a combination of wishful thinking and adrenaline.

By the time we'd met up with Lara for lunch, I was starting to have my own doubts, but Lara was clearly so buzzed about what had happened, it was infectious. Lucas asked her if she felt that energy every time she did a spell or a ritual as part of her Wicca practice. At first she hedged a bit, but then she acknowledged that while she had experienced similar *kinds* of things, it had never been that intense before. In fact, she seemed a bit alarmed by the intensity of the experience. But then she pointed out that it makes sense, because before she was a solo practitioner, and this time we were four people working in concert. So it probably multiplied all our energy together.

Lucas wanted to know if this made us all officially witches now. Or if there's a different word for male witches. I jumped in and suggested "wizard," and Caleb thought maybe "magician" or "sorcerer," but Lara said there have been male witches for as long as witchcraft has been around, which is basically forever, and they're also called witches for the most part.

"But you can't actually become a witch overnight," she clarified. "It's not like it is in the movies, where anyone can say some magic words and suddenly sparks come shooting out their fingers." She talked about how real witches spend years studying and learning and practicing their craft. And that it's not only about getting wishes granted—it's also about honoring the natural world and the forces of the universe. You can't take without giving back.

I'm not stating it very well here, and it all sounds obvious now, but her explanation piqued my interest even more. Suddenly I had *all* these questions for her, as did Lucas and Caleb. But right then one of the mega-church girls interrupted us. She's not one of the super popular ones, but some freshman whom I think might be the little sister of one of the Queen Bees of the school. She obviously had been eavesdropping on our conversation from a nearby table, and when she approached us all shy and nervous at first, I turned to her, wondering if she needed help with something. She stepped forward and, in a squeaky little voice barely above a whisper, quoted some Bible verse at us: "Those who follow witchcraft will be put into the lake of fire and sulfur, which is the second death."

Then she plopped a Bible in the middle of our table and ran away as if the Devil himself were after her.

As soon as I realized what she was doing, I felt a wave of fury flare up in me. Why can't people leave us alone? They have no right to spy on us and force their beliefs down our throats.

Lara must have sensed me tense up, because she put a calming hand on my arm. I've heard people say all kinds of things to Lara over the years, including every Bible verse relating to witchcraft at least three times over. She never loses her cool. I hope I can be that poised one day.

Luckily Lucas broke the somber mood by jumping up from the table and yelling after her, "You'd better run, before we turn you into a toad!" Then he let out a Hollywood-witchy cackle.

Lara tried to give him a hard time about it, saying that kind of thing wasn't exactly helping the image of Wicca in the popular imagination. But I could tell she was a little pleased, too. It's not like those people are going to listen to rational, reasonable arguments.

SATURDAY, OCTOBER 8, 1:30 P.M.

I haven't updated here in a little while. There hasn't been all that much to say. I've been in a much better mood since we did Lara's ritual, less angry and frustrated over every little thing. Which means I have less reason to journal.

I'm more at peace with the Book of Shadows, too. I no longer feel like I'm unworthy of it. It helps that I'm not trying to force it to be a diary anymore. Lara was right—if the book is capable of having a desire or a destiny, then it must want to be a Book of Shadows.

But even though I still haven't written in the book, that doesn't necessarily mean that I've pushed it aside. In fact, lately I take it out every day before bed and I run my fingers over the elaborate tracing on the cover, admiring the glowing gold paint on the pages' edges and how they catch the light as I rifle them.

Even Lara's strange, curly handwriting on the first page seems beautiful and thrilling now.

The only trouble is, I don't know what I have to add to the book. I'm not familiar with a lot of spells, like Lara is, so I'm not sure where another one will come from—let alone enough to fill up the whole volume. But I'll deal with that some other time. In any case, I'm not too worried. The current situation feels right, and I'm in no rush to fill the book with nonsense just so I can say I've done it. When the right time and the right spell come, I'll know.

MONDAY, OCTOBER 10, 6:30 P.M.

Well, I've added something new to the Book of Shadows, and sooner than I expected to. I know I said in my last entry that I was happy to wait until the right inspiration came to me. And I held to that for a little while, but for some reason I woke up today feeling different. I took out the Book of Shadows in the morning like I usually do, but instead of feeling calmed by running my hands over all its clean, white pages, I started to feel antsy and energized and a little frantic. I don't know why. It was getting to me that this is supposedly my book, but so far the only person who had written in it is Lara. And well, Caleb, too, even though I tore that sheet out. But I hadn't even written a word. It felt wrong, somehow—I started to worry that in some way, maybe the book belonged to them more than to me. And I needed to do something to make my mark on the book, so it would know that it was mine.

Which doesn't exactly make sense. What does the book care who it belongs to, or how they use it? But once this idea filled my head I couldn't get rid of it. But I still didn't have any spells to add to it, or really any idea what someone might put in a Book of Shadows. So I decided to bring it into school with me again and maybe stop by the library at some point to do some research on witchcraft. I suppose I could have borrowed some books from Lara, or even asked her to give me another spell. But this time I wanted it to feel like it was *my* work, not something borrowed from my friend. That was my plan, until something unusual happened. . . .

I was in history class, where Mr. Peters was droning on and on about the Inquisition or something . . . I'm not sure, only that the lecture was even more boring than usual. I was trying to take notes, but my mind kept wandering and I was having trouble staying focused. At last the bell rang, and as I was collecting my things I noticed that I'd been doodling aimlessly for the past God knows how long. But that's not the strange part—a lot of my class notebooks are filled with doodles. Completely normal. But this time I wasn't doodling in my class notebook. At some point, I must have taken the Book of Shadows out of my bag, opened it up to a blank page, and started drawing. So now I have this random drawing in the middle of my precious book.

I'm not quite sure what to think about this. At first I was horrified at what I'd done. After all that time worrying about what was appropriate to write in the book, my first real contribution winds up being some thoughtless drawing? Immediately I started panicking and making plans to tear the page out again, like I did when Caleb wrote in it. But then I remembered that horrible sense that came over me last time I removed a page from the book. Like it was angry with me. Plus there was all that blood! Which I'm sure was a coincidence, but it was still a bit unnerving.

It's more than that, though. Looking at the drawing itself . . . this isn't an ordinary drawing. I catch myself doodling in the margins of my notebooks all the time, but never anything like this before. Usually it's geometric patterns, intricate mazes or swirl designs that grow and grow until either they fill the page or the class ends.

But this is different. It reminds me of all the little beasts tangled together on the cover of the Book of Shadows. Other than the cover, I have no idea where the inspiration for this drawing could have come from. It worries me a little that something like this was hiding in some subconscious corner of my brain. Makes you wonder what else might be camping out in there.

Perhaps it has something to do with what that freshman girl said the other day, about practitioners of witchcraft being dragged down to hell. Even though I never gave much thought to hell or the Devil before, for some reason her words spooked me a bit. Sometimes they pop into my mind, and this guilty chill surges through me, as if I really think I'm going to be dragged down to hell. Maybe because, for the first time, I've actually dabbled in something that could be considered witchcraft. Lately I find myself wondering what it would be like. You know, to burn for all eternity, surrounded by demons and lost souls.

That's silly, though. It's only a drawing; it has nothing to do with hellfire and brimstone. I can't let those mega-church ass-holes get to me with all their ridiculous moralizing.

I've decided I'm going to leave the picture in the Book of Shadows for now. But I have to be more careful with that book! I don't want to accidentally find myself writing shopping lists in it.

WEDNESDAY, OCTOBER 19, 10:32 P.M.

Not much to report since last time. I suppose I tend to reach for my diary when I have something to complain about, or document some kind of chaos that needs sorting out. Right now, things are going pretty well, which means I don't have that much to say.

I've gotten 92 percent or above on my last six history quizzes. And before that, my average hovered around 76 percent. What changed? I'd love to say it's because I've been studying harder or paying more attention in class, but if anything it's the opposite. My focus in class is off, I'm more distracted than ever, and I've wound up doing three more drawings in the Book of Shadows instead of taking notes. The only way I can explain it is, I've been guessing right on the multiple choice questions. That has to be it, right? Not that I'm complaining.

The only thing I do have to complain about is, I haven't been sleeping well lately. I don't think it's insomnia—I fall asleep easily every night and I don't wake up until my alarm goes off. It's more about the bad dreams I've been having, though I don't really remember them. There's no story or specific fear to these dreams, rather a vague sense of something dark and threatening, barely out of sight. What I do remember is being restless. For some reason I keep trying to move around so I can see this eerie presence. Even though I know whatever it is would be scary and horrible, I *need* to see it. But whatever it is keeps slipping away from me.

Oh, that reminds me, for some reason my little art project has been found out. And I have a fan! I was flipping through the Book of Shadows one day at Lucas's house after school, and Lucas caught a glimpse of one of my drawings. He made me stop and asked if I would show it to him. I hesitated at first—it's a dreadful creature—hunchbacked and scaly, with its skull cracked like an eggshell. What kind of twisted mind even comes up with an image like that? I was afraid he'd think I was seriously disturbed. But he stared at it awhile and then asked me if I'd drawn it. I told him I had, and he was clearly impressed. "It could be on some metal band's album cover," were his exact words, I believe. And, if you know how Lucas feels about heavy metal bands, this is pretty much the greatest compliment he could give. He even called me an artist.

The idea that anyone would think of me as an artist left me surprisingly . . . proud. I've never really had a special talent before, or anything that made me stand out in a positive way. But maybe I've had this hidden talent within me, waiting for something to break it free, and it took my new interest in magic to release it. It's not the kind of thing an art teacher would approve of (especially not at *this* school), but there might be other people, people like Lucas, who would appreciate my style.

Of course Lucas also said it was the kind of thing that would give him nightmares if he hung it up on his wall. And though that might seem like a criticism to most people, knowing Lucas the way I do, I don't believe he meant it that way. He's completely obsessed with death metal, horror movies, and zombie video games, so "nightmare fodder" is pretty much his definition of cool.

I wonder if that's where my own nightmares come from. If I'm dreaming versions of the things I've been drawing. But in that case, are my bad dreams inspired by my drawings, or the other way around? Or are they both being influenced by some other source?

Either way, I'm glad I got a chance to bond with Lucas over my new hobby. I've never had that much of a direct relationship with him before, even though I hang out with him every day. He's always been Caleb's friend, really. But now I feel like we have a kind of connection.

FRIDAY, OCTOBER 21, 8:42 P.M.

Lara was in a super good mood today—bouncing off the walls—
and I couldn't figure out why, so finally I asked and she said, "Oh
my God, Mel, I got my period today and I feel like I've grown
wings." Not a normal reaction to getting one's period, I know,
but apparently she and Caleb had a bit of an "accident" a few
weeks ago. She was late and she was starting to worry that she
might be pregnant.

I can't even imagine—with Caleb's ultrareligious parents,
who knows what they might do if they found out something like
that. It would definitely be the end of Caleb and Lara's relationship. Sneaking around is already part of the norm for them since
Caleb's parents aren't exactly thrilled about him dating the town
witch. No doubt they'd blame her. Say she did it on purpose to
trap him, all because the Devil is whispering in her ear.

FRIDAY, OCTOBER 2I, II:22 P.M.

A minute ago I was finishing up another drawing in the Book of
Shadows, and I this incredible headache hit me out of nowhere.
Well, not a headache exactly . . . It's hard to describe. It was more
like an uncomfortable, angsty feeling—more of an emotional
pain than a physical one. It moved to my eyes, and everything
went dark and blurry around the edges. I had trouble focusing.
If anything the headache reminded me of those bad dreams I've
been having. I don't know why that would be.

How strange! It seems to have passed as quickly as it came on.

Suddenly Lara grabbed my arm, saying, "It must be thanks to the spell we did!" It took me a moment to figure out what she was talking about. "You think you're not pregnant because we performed a good luck spell?" I laughed. "It's not that unusual for someone to be a couple weeks late, Lara."

She shrugged her shoulders, a smile breaking on her face before she walked—though the better word might be *skipped*—happily away.

MONDAY, OCTOBER 24, 3:46 P.M.

I feel awful. Mainly because I'm covered in bruises, but I know it's mostly guilt. I swore I wasn't going to do this anymore—that I wasn't going to lose control.

In my defense, the girl I hit was really asking for it. But that's no excuse. I feel as if I've disappointed everyone, including myself, but especially Lara.

It all came out of nowhere. Lara and I were talking about her pregnancy scare, and since it's kind of a private topic we were leaning toward each other so no one else would hear. Then some Queen Bees came sauntering over to us, giggling. "I want you to know that I am praying for you every day," said Betty Fillmore. A hot feeling started bubbling in my blood, but Lara whispered for me to ignore them. So I took a deep breath, hoping it would calm me down.

But when Betty said, "I'm praying that you find Jesus and he saves you from being a lez," that's when I snapped.

I don't even remember exactly what happened. My vision whited out and a dark rage rose up inside me. Suddenly I wasn't thinking at all. The next thing I knew, people were shrieking and Betty was under me, her face scratched and bleeding. I don't know how long I might have kept it up. But what I do remember is that the one thing that brought me back to reality was Lara's voice, low and soft, telling me to relax and let Betty go.

All the energy drained out of me and I sagged down on the floor, shaking violently. Lara helped me up and we walked outside. She then called my mom, who came and took me home. I crawled right into bed and slept for hours.

But now that I'm awake, I'm starting to worry about what kind of trouble I must be in. I'm definitely going to get suspended again, at least. My parents are going to be pissed! They'll probably force me to see a psychologist or take pills.

I'm such an idiot. Why did I even do it? I don't care if people think I'm a lesbian—it's no worse than what people already think of me. And it's not like I think there's anything wrong with it.

I guess it has more to do with my relationship with Lara. We've been friends for a while now, but I still feel like she's cooler, prettier, and smarter than me. I worry all the time that I'm suffocating her with my friendship, and that one day she'll move on and forget all about me. If she thinks that I'm coming on to her, or that I want some kind of romantic relationship with her, that might drive her away.

I understand that this is *my* insecurity. Something I need to figure out and deal with—but in a less violent way. What I did to Betty—it was almost as if an outside force stepped inside me and took over.

MONDAY, OCTOBER 24, 4:06 P.M.

I finished another drawing. I'm starting to get oddly attached to these odd-looking creatures. At first they creeped me out, but now they feel more friendly.

Lara told me a while ago that I should write in my diary whenever I feel angry or violent, and that would channel my negative emotions in a more productive way. But that's never helped much at all. These drawings, though—they seem to do the trick. There's something soothing about zoning out and letting these creatures grow out of my pen. I don't have to think about it at all—I put my pen on the paper and it's almost like they draw themselves.

MONDAY, OCTOBER 24, 7:09 P.M.

Lara came by to visit a couple of hours ago. I'm so relieved she isn't mad at me—of all the consequences to my actions, that would have been the worst. She did lecture me a bit about violence never being the answer. Of course I know that. I tried to explain myself to her. It's not a question of not knowing the right choices to make. The problem is, it's not easy to think about right and wrong in the heat of the moment. When something makes me angry, I'm not thinking through the best, most rational response—I'm reacting with my heart, not my head.

I know I need to control myself better, and I *have* been. Sometimes I slip up, though.

The good news is, I don't seem to be in any trouble! I can't explain it. A dozen people must have seen me go after Betty, including the lunchroom monitor. Plus leaving early should have earned me a detention. But Lara says that after I left, everyone acted like nothing happened. Now that I think about it, even my mom didn't ask me why I needed to be picked up. She assumed I was feeling sick, and I didn't correct her.

That seems strange but I'm not going to question it. Sometimes you get lucky.

We talked some more about what happened, and Lara said she couldn't blame me all that much, since those girls were being such idiots. Then she added, "Mel, I want you know . . . if you *are* gay, you can tell me. You know that, right?"

I didn't know what to say. I love her so much for being the kind of person who can be completely chill and accepting at the idea that her best friend might be gay. But I couldn't express that emotion without it sounding like I'm trying to hit on her. And I'm not! It's not like I want to steal her away from Caleb, or get married, or make out with her. I'm happy with our relationship the way it is now. I hope Lara can understand that and not worry that I'm expecting anything more.

I did at least manage to babble something about not liking girls in that way. And she seemed to get it, so I felt as if I'd handled the whole situation pretty well. But then Lara made everything even more awkward, asking, "In that case, are there any boys you like?"

I know this conversation comes up between most female friends, but Lara and I don't discuss romance and flirting and sex very much. We've talked about her and Caleb, especially when they were first getting together, but when it comes to me . . . I don't know. We tend to avoid that issue. Almost anything in the world is more interesting, to be honest.

I didn't know how to answer her question. I said, "No, not

especially." But when she said, "Well, if you were interested, I can think of someone who is pretty interested in you." I got this horrible sinking feeling in my stomach. *Oh no, it's starting, I'm going to have to deal with this.* Curious, though, I asked who. Lara teased and hinted for a while before finally saying, "What do you think of Lucas?"

Well, what do I think of Lucas? He's nice and smart and funny. I like him. (*And cute!*, pointed out Lara. Okay, if she says so.) "Are you interested?" said Lara.

"I don't know," I told her, which is probably misleading, even though it's the truth.

Now that I'm home alone without the Spanish Inquisition in my face (Oh, hey, I guess I did learn something in that class after all!), what *do* I think of Lucas? I was flattered when he complimented my drawings. And though he can be a jerk sometimes when Caleb gets him going, he's a decent guy. We have a lot in common—it's nice to have an ally against all those megachurch Queen Bees who run the school.

Plus, there would be definite perks to having a boyfriend. My parents would be happy. I'd have something to do when Lara and Caleb start making out on the couch. And it would be nice if those obnoxious girls would stop insisting I'm a lesbian and making awkward insinuations around Lara.

Are those good enough reasons to have a boyfriend? I don't think so.

TUESDAY, OCTOBER 25, 5:45 P.M.

Even though things are going well right now, I find that I am nervous and jumpy all the time. Maybe it's leftover energy from that fight I was in, or maybe it's anxiety over what Lara said about Lucas. The only thing that calms me down is making more of those drawings in the Book of Shadows.

It's a bit unsettling, though, that I never set out to create a new drawing. I'll be staring off into space one moment, and then I blink and find the book in my hands and a new drawing there, and sometimes minutes or hours have passed. The drawings are getting more elaborately eccentric, too, but I like them. I made one the other day that was a cross between a bird and a dragon, but with tentacles where its mouth should be.

I am a little worried about how my new hobby is interfering with the rest of my life, though. First it was scary dreams, and now and then I convince myself that I've seen a dark, undulating form in a corner even when I'm awake. Though I can never be sure. I've never seen anything directly. It's this disquieting impression I have occasionally, at the edge of my vision, or when I glance at a cloud or a shadow. At times I feel like something is watching me. When I turn to look at it, it always turns out to be nothing, of course. But when I close my eyes and try to picture what I almost saw, all I remember is undulating bodies and inhuman faces.

I don't know why this is happening, but I figure it must be some kind of stress reaction. At least it's distracting me from thinking about whatever is going on with Lucas.

WEDNESDAY, OCTOBER 26, 3:55 P.M.

Well! So much for avoiding thinking about Lucas for a while. I thought I'd have some time, at least, to chew over my feelings on this subject, but he accosted me today at lunch. Maybe Lara is right about him developing an interest?

But he didn't ask me out or try to kiss me. Instead he told me that he had recently won the lead in the school play, which was why he seemed so nervous. *So* not what I was expecting! Shocked, I couldn't do anything but stare at him. That made him even more nervous. "It's really lame, isn't it?" he said.

I laughed, more out of relief than anything else. I didn't want him to think I was laughing at *him*, so I quickly added, "No, that's incredible!" I'd had no idea he was even into theater. He'd never mentioned anything about it before. It definitely seemed a little out of the blue for him to be suddenly cast as the lead.

Apparently Lucas feels the same way about his theater success. He'd never performed before, or had any interest in the activity. But his English teacher, who runs the school's theater, asked him a few weeks ago to stay after class. Lucas thought he was going to get in trouble for horsing around and cracking jokes. Instead the teacher said, "I've had my eye on you for a while. You have a great energy about you. Have you ever thought about performing?" And he invited him to audition for the play.

Figuring it wouldn't amount to anything, Lucas auditioned to see what it was like. Believing he'd, at the most, get cast in some tiny part with two lines, he won the lead!

So . . . he asked me if he should take it. I don't know why he'd ask me, except maybe he was nervous that Caleb or Lara might tease him about it and make him feel a fool for being drawn to such jejune pursuits. Of course I told him he should go for it and that I was sure he'd be an outstanding actor.

I was overwhelmingly relieved after all that, because the thing I had been so nervous about turned out to be nothing, and instead I was able to make my friend happy in this whole other way, and it all felt like it worked out gorgeously.

Oh, there was one other thing, though. I thought our conversation was over, but as I was moving to leave, Lucas stopped me and pulled me into a hug. I stood there in shock, listening while he thanked me. But that doesn't mean anything, right? A hug can be friendly. Unless he meant it to be more than friendly. . . . How is anyone ever supposed to interpret these social cues?

FRIDAY, OCTOBER 28, 4:28 P.M.

Maybe I should take a little break from working on these drawings. Yeah, they help calm me down and stop my thoughts for a while, but they are starting to get under my skin. The minute I close the book and put it away, I start seeing them now . . . never directly in my vision, but in every shadow and every window reflection. . . . Today I was touching up my eyeliner in the school bathroom and I could have sworn I saw something creeping around in the background of the mirror. Some globby, squiddy creature with a dozen staring eyes. I wonder if this is a common thing that happens to artsy people? I wish someone could reassure me that I'm not going crazy—it's a bit scary.

I think it's best if I stop for a while and try to find some other ways to relax. The problem is, I don't even realize I'm drawing in the book half the time. How do you quit something you don't even know you're doing? I could leave the damn Book of Shadows at home. That would make the most sense, wouldn't it? But I don't know if I want to do that.

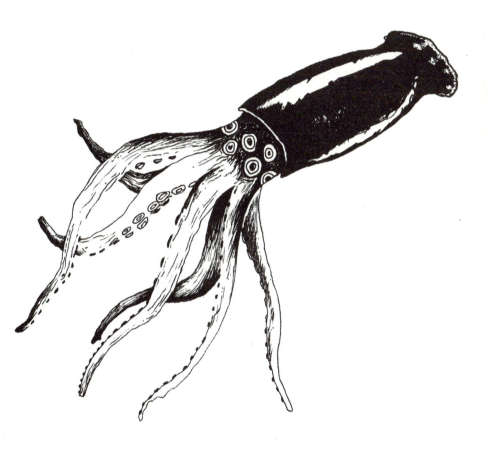

TUESDAY, NOVEMBER 1, 3:18 P.M.

I can't believe it. Caleb got a phone call earlier today, out of the blue—he's being recruited to the state university on a football scholarship. HE DOESN'T EVEN PLAY FOOTBALL. I mean, he did last year, but he quit the team. I may not know a ton about sports, but I'm pretty sure they don't hand out scholarships to quitters. But this scout says he saw him play last year and thought he had exceptional promise, and wants to offer him a free ride scholarship. A. FREE. RIDE.

And the timing is what makes it even more incredible, because last night Caleb had a huge fight with his dad over where he is going to college next year. His father is on the board of a local Christian college and thinks it's a no-brainer for Caleb to attend, but Caleb doesn't want to give up any more of his life to that church. But his father has been saying he wouldn't pay for anywhere else, so Caleb was stuck—either follow his father's demands, or skip college altogether. His best hope was to work for a few years to save up money for the college of his choice.

Only today, he gets this call, which obviously changes everything. Now he could go to a really good school and not have to pay a dime! Which means he is completely independent from his father's demands. It's incredible! And it solves all Caleb's problems.

Though I never saw him play, Caleb admits that he was never that great. He was good, but not the team's star player. One reason he quit the team was his certainty that he'd never be good enough to earn a scholarship. He simply wasn't in that league. Or was he? Hell.

Is this all because of our good luck spell? My grades, Lara's pregnancy-scare, Lucas's audition, and now this . . . It's starting to look more like a pattern than a coincidence. But can it really be that the four of us made this happen?

I'm going over to Lucas's now to celebrate with the others. It's exhilarating to think we could have that kind of power. A little scary, too. . . . It's a good thing we picked such a harmless spell. Who knows what could have happened if we had wished for something bad?

TUESDAY, NOVEMBER 1, 7:38 P.M.

I'm back from Lucas's. Of course all we could talk about was the good luck spell and if it was real. It has to be! It's the only possible explanation.

The others agree with me, and Lara, Lucas, and I were beside ourselves with wonder at the idea that we actually did real magic. Caleb, however, seemed oddly quiet and subdued about our dalliance with the supernatural. Which is surprising, because his luck has been the best out of all of us. That football scholarship? It's incredible. It's such a perfect solution to all his problems. No way that could be due to ordinary luck.

At first I thought Caleb didn't want to admit that it was magic because he's overly invested in his antireligious world-view. Thanks to his history with his father and the mega-church, it would be no surprise if Caleb insisted that every supernatural event must be superstition. Turns out that wasn't it at all. When I finally asked him about it, he didn't deny the magic. He would only say the situation made him nervous.

So then Lucas pointed out that Caleb hadn't had a problem with it earlier, when the rest of us were having good luck. And Caleb said, "Yeah, that's when I thought it wasn't real." All the previous incidents, he had convinced himself were coincidence. But this latest one seemed too strange to deny.

"So what if it is real?" said Lara. "Would that be bad? Don't you want the universe to be a beautiful, magical place?"

But Caleb wouldn't budge. He said that we'd be better off if we knew more about where this power was coming from. Personally, I think he is being ridiculous. Who cares where the magic comes from? Lara, always needing to accommodate Caleb's feelings, tried to act sympathetic. She said his worries were reasonable, and that maybe we would all feel better about what we were doing if we knew more about where the book came from.

Then she looked at me, because of course I should have the answer to that question. But I froze. I couldn't bear to tell her that I stole the book from her favorite store, but I didn't want to lie, either. So I stood there silently, tears forming in my eyes as she prodded me, demanding to know why I wouldn't answer. I was about to run out of the room, when Caleb got some emergency text from his dad and Caleb said he had to take everyone home right away. That must have distracted Lara, because she let the subject drop after that.

I hope she forgets about it. I really don't want to tell her where the book came from.

TUESDAY, NOVEMBER 1, 10:32 P.M.

What a strange evening! I was in my room doing homework when I got a text from Caleb. He was outside my house in his car, and he told me to come down. A little unusual since Caleb and I don't hang out without Lara there. But I was curious, so I went.

Turns out, his dad didn't have any emergency this afternoon. Caleb made up the whole thing to get Lara off my back. That was . . . unexpected. I'm so used to thinking of Caleb as a jerk, it never occurred to me that he might actually be looking out for me. But he could see how uncomfortable Lara was making me with her questions, and he faked the text to get her to leave me alone.

He asked me what I was trying to hide from her, and I told him. I didn't mean to tell anyone, but somehow it's easier to tell Caleb about my bad behavior than Lara. It's not that Lara is judgmental, exactly—it's that she never seems to have any personal struggles with morality. For her, the world is a simple place where every action is divided into right and wrong, and all you have to do is pick "good" instead of "bad." Even when other people accuse her of being evil, she never doubts herself for a moment. It's as if she was born with a moral compass that always points her in the right direction and guides all her behavior. It's one of the things I love about her, but it also has a tendency to make me feel small and unsure about myself.

Caleb, on the other hand—Caleb only has to ask a question and I want to spill out all my most secret thoughts to him. It's not just me, either. Caleb has a talent for making people say things they'd never say, and do things they'd never do.

It's not *mind control*. Rather, he has an uncanny gift of making you feel as if you are the only person who exists in the world—the only one who matters. That you are more important to him in that specific moment than anyone else. His voice goes soft but insistent, and his eyes get really intense—I think he must have picked it up from his father's preaching. I've seen him work this magic a couple of times, usually directed toward teachers or administrators, but I'd never felt its effect before. Even though I knew exactly what he was doing, I couldn't help thinking, *People would go to war for a voice like that*. It's not that I *couldn't* resist him—more that I suddenly didn't want to. If his dad does anything like this in church, it's no wonder he draws such a massive, devoted crowd.

When Caleb asked me where I'd gotten the book, I didn't hesitate to tell him about how I stole it from White Rabbit. He wasn't shocked or disappointed the way Lara would have been.

He told me not to worry, that he'd keep my secret. He even told me some stories about his own shoplifting experiences when he was younger, which made me feel less awful about it. Then he asked if it would be okay for him to go to White Rabbit alone to ask about the book. He promised not to use my name—he's only going to describe the book and ask the owner if he remembers where it came from.

I don't love the idea. Honestly I want to forget about the whole incident and move forward with life. But he kept pressing the point, and finally I told him if it would make him feel better about using the book, I was okay with it. I suppose it can't really do any harm. And even I'm a little curious about where this strange book came from.

THURSDAY, NOVEMBER 3, 10:32 P.M.

It looks like Caleb's plan worked. At lunch today he told us that he had found the previous owner of the Book of Shadows.

Predictably, Lara and Lucas wanted to know how he'd figured it out, and all I could do was silently pray that Caleb wouldn't give me away. But he remembered his promise. He told them that he "has his ways" and made a big joke out of it, saying that he preferred to keep an air of mystery than to reveal all his secrets. Thankfully, Lara and Lucas bought it. I'm sure Caleb's natural charm helped persuade the two of them. It's impressive how he can direct a conversation whichever way he likes, without any objections.

Anyway, it turns out the book came from a woman named Hecate Blum. Yes, really! Hecate, like in *Macbeth*. And Lara says it's the name of a Wiccan goddess. I can hardly believe it!

I've never met any witch aside from Lara, and I never pictured witchcraft as something adults might do.

Caleb called her up and asked if we could meet with her this weekend. I'm kind of nervous—given what we've already accomplished with the Book of Shadows, I can only imagine what a real witch with a lifetime's worth of study and training could do.

SATURDAY, NOVEMBER 5, 3:22 P.M.

I'm back from our meeting with Hecate. Who actually goes by "Kate" these days.

That should be a pretty good tip-off of how the meeting went: anticlimactic, to say the least. But interesting, nonetheless.

We drove out to the address she'd given Caleb over the phone, and I was seriously expecting some kind of ramshackle old mansion out of a storybook. So imagine my disappointment when we pulled into the driveway and it turned out to be an ordinary split-level ranch house. There was a horse in the side yard (but that's not really unusual around here), and a couple of kids playing touch football out front. The opposite of spooky.

When Hecate came to the door, she was wearing mom jeans and an old sweatshirt, and seemed moderately annoyed at the intrusion, though she invited us in for tea. We all sat down at her breakfast bar, none of us knowing quite what to say—how on earth could this ordinary looking woman be the source of my mysterious book?

But after a couple of tentative questions, Caleb coaxed the story out of her. Hecate is no witch—she was very clear about that. But her parents were—or thought they were. That's how she wound up with the name. Her parents became interested in magic and the "mystic arts" back in the 1960s and started calling themselves witches. They even started a coven with a few other "hippies and weirdos" in the area. A surprising revelation. The mega-church dominates this town, and it's hard to imagine that only a few decades ago, there were *witches* and an actual *coven* around here.

But apparently it was all pretty serious. Hecate's father started collecting books on witchcraft, and gradually became obsessed with acquiring the rarest and most obscure volumes, sometimes even traveling to Europe, following up on even the flimsiest rumors of powerful grimoires for sale.

Hecate was clearly still pretty bitter about growing up in such an odd household. She said they never had much money since they spent all their time and resources on exploring witchcraft, and neither of her parents ever bothered to find steady jobs. Her father was convinced that his fortune was due to change any day, if only he could find the right magic to bend the universe to his whims.

When Hecate was little, she bought into this story, and thoroughly believed that her parents were powerful magicians, similar to all the fairy tales she had read. But as she grew older, she realized that nothing about her life was very magical at all. Eventually she came to the conclusion that it was all a seductive fantasy. When things went well, her parents credited it to their spell craft. When everything went wrong, they always had a million excuses—jealous witches interfering in their work, or a bad translation that led to a wrong ingredient in a potion, or the wrong energy during a ritual. Finally Hecate had to accept that none of it was ever real—that her parents had thrown away their entire lives on an illusion.

That, she explained, was why she agreed to meet with us. She wanted to help us see the truth before our lives were ruined by our delusions, as her parents' had been.

Needless to say, Lara wasn't too thrilled with this conversation. She tried to leave at one point, saying the whole thing was cruel and offensive to her belief system, but Caleb convinced her to stay and hear the woman out. Lara tried to argue with her a few times, and point out all the evidence we had of real magic. But Hecate had an answer for all her objections. She explained that once you perform a good luck spell, you're expecting good things to happen, so subconsciously you *do* things to make the good things happen. She also mentioned something she called "confirmation bias." It's when you want something to be true, so you only notice the evidence that supports it, and you ignore everything that contradicts it.

I didn't know what to say to any of that. The effects of our luck spell seemed *so* real. But it was hard to make Hecate see that. There was nothing we could point to that couldn't possibly have some other explanation. And it's true that she'd been around witchcraft and sorcery a lot more than we had. I wanted to back Lara up, but eventually I couldn't help wondering if Hecate was right.

I asked her what wound up happening to her parents in the

end. "They muddled along, surviving by the skin of their teeth," she answered. Then one day someone died—she didn't know if it was a family member or some old rich eccentric they had met through their magical studies, but he left her parents a lot of money. But what should have been a boon to them made everything worse. Her father became convinced that his magical explorations had at last born fruit, that this was the evidence he was looking for. He committed himself more than ever before to his occult practices, to the point where even her mom thought he had lost his senses.

Her father died around that time in a car wreck that Hecate suspected was really a suicide. After that, her life became more normal. Her mother moved all his books into a locked room and refused to talk about him or their metaphysical studies for the rest of her life. Once her mom died, Hecate had to have the door forced open before she could sell their house. She found all the books and she was going to burn them, but her husband convinced her that was silly and superstitious. They figured she might as well at least make some money off her parents' hobby, so she sold the books to various shops and dealers around the state, including a few to White Rabbit.

And that's how the Book of Shadows came to me. A pretty sad story, all things considered, and not at all as romantic or exciting as I had been picturing. I'm worried now that maybe Hecate is right—that we're on the same path her parents were, desperately looking for signs that magic is real, and falling so in love with the fantasy that we've lost touch with reality.

SUNDAY, NOVEMBER 6, 4:52 P.M.

It seems we're going to do another spell? I'm not sure I see the point. After everything Hecate told us . . . I thought we all agreed that we were seeing what we wanted to see with the luck spell, and it wasn't really magical after all. But apparently some of the others aren't so sure.

Lara, in particular, isn't ready to accept that the whole thing was in our heads. I can understand that. For me and the boys, this was all a fun way to blow off an afternoon or two. For Lara, this is her religion. I can't blame her for refusing to abandon it so easily.

But Caleb, for all his earlier nervousness, is now pretty adamantly in Hecate's school of thought. He started arguing with Lara, telling her she was being silly and irrational, and the fight was starting to get pretty nasty. To keep the peace, Lucas suggested we perform another spell—this time as a kind of test, to prove to ourselves that the good luck from the previous spell was a fluke.

I wasn't into the idea. I told him, what's to stop the same thing from happening again? We do a spell, and then subconsciously convince ourselves that it worked, like Hecate said. Lucas said we'd have to pick a better spell this time—one with clearer results, nothing that could be left open to interpretation.

I said fair enough and suggested levitating broomsticks, or transforming teacups into mice. We'd definitely know if those worked. But Lara said there aren't really any spells like that, except in movies.

That's when Lucas suggested the love spell.

Caleb was against it at first. He pointed out that love is no better than luck, in terms of being measurable and verifiable. If you put a spell on someone to love you, who's to say they wouldn't have loved you anyway?

So Lucas suggested picking someone really unlikely. Someone who couldn't possibly be interested without some kind of supernatural intervention. That would be a good test.

That's when I got nervous. Especially when Lucas wouldn't say who he had in mind. He insisted it would make a better experiment if we didn't know, so our expectations wouldn't bias the results. I looked across the room at Lara, and I could see that she had the same thought as I did. *Was Lucas planning to cast his love spell on me?*

That's kind of sketchy. If he wants to date me, why not ask me out, like a normal person? Maybe because he thinks I'd say no. Which . . . yes, that's true. I would. Because I don't want to date him.

Shouldn't that be the end of the story? I don't like the idea of being tricked or trapped into dating him. That's a terrible thing to do to someone.

So why didn't I say that to Lucas? I don't know. I was going to tell him. I was going to put my foot down and veto the spell. I mean, it's my book in the end, isn't it? Ultimately it should be my choice what goes in it. But Lara was so excited about the idea. She thinks Lucas and I would make a good couple, and that this would be a cute way for us to get together—I don't think she's thought about it much beyond that. And I didn't want to be a spoilsport when everyone else was having fun.

I don't relish the idea of being everyone's little science experiment, but . . . what does it matter, really? The magic isn't real, so it's nothing but fun and games anyway. I didn't see any point in making a big deal out of it, so I went along with the idea.

Still, even once everyone was on board, we had the problem of figuring out *what* spell to do. Lara said she knew of a couple, but she needed to go home and look it up in her books. Lucas was impatient, though, so he quickly pulled one up on his phone. Lara didn't like that at all—she kept talking about how important it was to use only spells from known and tested sources or else you might get all kinds of unexpected results. But Lucas rolled his eyes, grabbed the book and started writing. So that settled that.

Spell for Awakening Desire

Procure a bulb from a blooming plant and inscribe
upon the base the name of your beloved.

In a darkened room, place five black candles
in a circle. In the middle, place the bulb in a glass vase.

Sprinkle sulfur powder on the bulb, then set it aflame.

Focus your energy & chant this phrase:

"In the name of Räum, as this flower blooms,
so too will love."

Repeat until the flame dies.

As the bulb grows and blossoms,
your beloved's heart will turn to you.

So mote it be.

WEDNESDAY, NOVEMBER 9, 8:10 P.M.

I'm seriously having second thoughts about this love spell, though I'm not sure how to back out at this point. It's not only my personal aversion to being some magical guinea pig—there's something else. I think the spell *changed* again.

I mean, I'm sure it did. Except . . . how can I be so sure? I feel like I'm losing my mind.

When I walked into Lucas's, earlier today, I found him all excited to start gathering together the ritual elements. And as I read through the spell, I . . . well, I could have sworn it was different from what Lucas wrote down the other day. And this time I was really paying attention, so I don't think I was confused. For a moment Lucas also questioned whether the spell was the same. But Lara pointed out that it was all in Lucas's handwriting, so who else could have written it? She tried to reassure me that this was simply cold feet, the same as she went through when we did the good luck spell. She convinced herself there was something wrong with the spell because she was nervous about performing it in front of an audience, and I'm doing the same thing this time.

I want to believe her argument, but I'm not sure. I know it's impossible, but I could swear I remember that on Sunday the spell said three red candles, not five black ones. And we were supposed to burn some herb—rosemary I think? Not sulfur. And I'm pretty sure the name we were invoking was Aphrodite, the goddess of love. I don't know who Räum is.

So I thought, okay, there's a way to settle this: Lucas found the spell online, right? Let's go back to that website and check what the book says against the original spell. Everyone rolled their eyes at me, but I insisted. Lucas threw a huge fuss because he couldn't find the page right away, and couldn't remember the name of the site he'd been looking on. He thought he was using the same search terms as before, but of course there were a million websites claiming to have love spells, so it was hard to figure out which one was the right one. "Look, let's drop it, okay?" he said.

But I wouldn't. And I know, I was coming across as kind of a fanatic at this point, but I felt something crawling inside of me that *had* to see this through. I knew I'd never trust this spell until I checked it. So I made Lucas look through his web history until we found the exact site he'd used yesterday. When he clicked on it, he got an error message. Which seemed suspicious to me! Lucas said I was being ridiculous—that it didn't mean anything except that their web server was down. Which, yes, I grant that is a totally reasonable explanation. But something felt wrong to me, and I still couldn't give up my search. I hit reload again and again, always getting that same error message. Then finally, on like the tenth time, it came through.

And it was the same spell that was in the Book of Shadows. Precisely the same.

I definitely felt like an idiot then. And more than a little embarrassed. At that point, I did back off and concede that I must have gotten caught up in my bad dreams last night and imagined the whole thing.

Because it's obviously been the same spell all along. I mean, it has to be, right? That's the only thing that makes any sense at all. This is my mind playing tricks on me because I get all worked up over nothing—same as those creeping creatures that haunt me every time I blink. Same as those peculiar drawings I do without knowing it, like I'm in some kind of trance. It's all me and my oddball brain.

But . . . what if they're wrong, and I'm right? I can't stop thinking about what that would mean. It would mean that . . . well, it means that the book itself is somehow changing not only the words we write in it, but the world itself. That this Book of Shadows has the power to change what's on a website hosted out of God knows where. And all without our asking it to or casting any spell.

But that's impossible. It's like Hecate predicted—it's way too easy to get carried away by the spookiness of the situation, and start seeing things that aren't there. I need to relax.

WEDNESDAY, NOVEMBER 9, 11:30 P.M.

Okay, I was getting out of control in that last entry, but I'm calmer now. And all thanks to the Book of Shadows, oddly enough.

One moment I was fretting alone in my bedroom, jumping at every noise and hallucinating strange creatures slithering along my walls. Then the next moment I was relaxed and focused and I actually laughed at how ridiculous I was being. That's when I looked down and realized the Book of Shadows was in my lap, and I'd added another drawing to it. I don't think I've ever done that outside of school before.

I know I was supposed to be taking a break, but it really feels good to be doing it again. I don't know why I was so worried about it before—they're harmless little doodles. I had almost convinced myself that there was some kind of spooky magic putting those images in my head, but our talk with Hecate reassured me about that. With all our talk of spells and enchantments, I got worked up over nothing. I was intoxicated by the drama of it all.

Anyway, being in this calmer mindset helped me realize how silly the whole thing was. The spell never changed! After all, the others all saw the spell Sunday and today, and I'm the only one who thought there was anything different about it.

Well . . . actually, now that I think about it, I sort of wonder if Caleb might have had the same thought. He was awfully quiet when the others were trying to convince me it was all in my head. But when I asked him flat out if he remembered it being any different Sunday, he shrugged and said no, it seemed the same to him.

I don't know, though. Caleb presents himself as an ultra-rationalist, but sometimes it seems like he hasn't completely given up on the miracles and prayers he was raised with. And when it comes to magic, especially, I think there's a part of him that wants to believe it's real, and another part that is deathly afraid it might be.

But even if it's true that Caleb still carries some vestigial beliefs from his church-going days, that still doesn't make it real. I have to be rational and scientific about this. I can't let myself get carried away, like I did the last time.

THURSDAY, NOVEMBER 10, 6:10 P.M.

Lucas still wanted to do the love spell, which meant driving around to assemble all the necessary supplies. According to the spell, we needed black candles, which we found in a New Age shop two towns away. We also needed sulfur powder, but Caleb remembered his parents used some to prevent mites on their pets. The last thing we needed was a tulip bulb, which Lucas dug up from his mom's garden when she wasn't looking. By then it was pretty late, though, so we agreed to put off the ritual itself until tomorrow.

I have to keep reminding myself that this is all for fun. Otherwise I start thinking about what would happen if it were real, which makes me anxious and queasy. I'll be relieved when this "experiment" is over and we can all admit that these magic spells have no effect in the real world.

FRIDAY, NOVEMBER 11, 12:20 P.M.

Everything's all set for the ritual after school today. I was feeling a bit apprehensive when I woke up, but then I drew another picture and I feel better now.

I don't know why the idea of doing this spell makes me so jumpy. If what Hecate told us is true, then none of this is real and it's all a game.

I guess there is a tiny part of me that thinks that it could be real. When I look back at my journal entry I wrote after our first ritual, it's clear that I felt *something*. Maybe it was all in my head, maybe it was some kind of group hypnosis, but the feeling itself was real and was very intense. I'm wondering whether I'll feel that again this time, or whether that only happens if you really believe in what you're doing.

To be honest, I'm not even sure how strong the feeling was

in the first place. I can see what I wrote, but the experience isn't fresh in my mind anymore. It's hard to know how powerful it really was, or whether we were all exaggerating a bit to ourselves and to one another.

Maybe part of it is that I'm worried that I'll *make* the spell come true by overthinking it. Lucas made a big deal out of not telling us who the spell was for, so it wouldn't affect the way we interpreted the results. But I'm pretty sure I've guessed who's name he is using—does that mean I might throw off the results of our experiment? Maybe the ritual will get under my skin somehow and convince me that I actually am in love with Lucas, even without any real magic.

That's a scary thought. But hopefully being aware of that possibility will make it less likely to happen.

FRIDAY, NOVEMBER 11, 10:23 P.M.

Well, we did it—we completed the love ritual. And now that it's over with, I'm even more anxious and uncertain about it than I was before.

Once Lucas got home from rehearsal, we started assembling all our ritual materials on the altar (which was actually Lucas's old coffee table, but whatever). Then of course Lucas insisted on being super secretive about carving the name of his "beloved" into the bulb. Caleb kept hassling him about who it was, but Lucas wouldn't tell anyone or let them see; and he made sure to place the bulb in the glass jar himself. I don't know. . . . I think if Caleb noticed the meaningful looks Lara kept giving me, or how badly I was blushing, he probably could have figured it out for himself. I have to admit, I'm nervous about what I've gotten myself into with this ritual.

After that we shut off all the lights so it was almost pitch dark in the basement. And when Lucas set fire to the sulfur powder, it glowed blue! That was probably the coolest part. Really eerie. And it left a curious black residue on the bulb.

Then we did the chanting thing for a while, finishing with Lara saying, "So mote it be."

Writing it out like that, it all sounds a little hokey. But now that we've done it again . . . I definitely don't think I exaggerated anything in my description from last time. That intensity I felt, the energy—it was unquestionably present this time too. But there was something different. A . . . quality. It's hard to describe, but if I had to put it into words, the energy of the first ritual was like that feeling you have on the first beautiful day of spring, when your body is thrumming with excitement, and everything good seems possible. It was like that feeling, multiplied by ten. But this time . . . this time it was more like the feeling when a storm that's been brewing all day finally breaks, and the wind howls so fiercely, and the rain beats down so hard, and you wonder if the whole town is going to be swept away. It's exciting but also a little scary.

I wonder if the others felt the same way, or if it was because I was uneasy about the whole thing from the beginning.

SATURDAY, NOVEMBER 12, 2:13 A.M.

Even after all the excitement today, I can't sleep. My mind keeps turning it over in my head. At first all I could really think about was how it felt in the moment to perform the ritual, and how the others felt about it. But now my mind keeps wandering back to that other question. . . . What if this ritual works? Or what if I somehow make it work by anticipating it and worrying about it?

I did wonder if there would be some crucial moment during the ritual when I felt some kind of switch flip in my heart, and I suddenly developed overpowering romantic feelings toward Lucas. Maybe that was naive, but in any case, I definitely didn't experience that. Then again, the good luck thing didn't hit us all at once, either.

What if I wake up tomorrow morning with all these new feelings for Lucas? I'm not sure I even know what that means.

I've never been in love, so it's all a mystery to me. I already like Lucas, and I can acknowledge that he's cute and nice and easy to talk to. But there's more to love and attraction than that. I have no experience with really *wanting* someone, the way Lara and Caleb want each other.

Would it really be so terrible? It could be interesting, to feel something I've never felt before. Plus, it might solve a lot of problems in my life. I wouldn't have to hear about my lack of a boyfriend at every family get together. I might feel more normal and accepted at school. And those mega-church Queen Bees . . . they might never love me, but they'd at least have to stop making obnoxious comments about me and Lara.

Still, there's something about the idea that's chilling. It might make my life easier, in some ways, to let another person take control of my thoughts, my emotions, my desires, but I wouldn't feel like *me* anymore. I'd be no better than a puppet on a string.

SATURDAY, NOVEMBER 12, 9:46 A.M.

Nothing much to report yet. The first thing I did this morning was check myself for . . . *symptoms*, I suppose you could say. Something new inside me that I'd never felt before. But I didn't encounter anything unusual. Then I wondered if maybe it had to be activated by the presence of Lucas, so I spent some time thinking about him. I even read over his old texts, and looked up a couple of photos online to see if they provoked those fluttery feelings other people describe having about their crushes. But there didn't seem to be anything new inside me.

I'm relieved, mostly—though maybe a tiny bit disappointed, too. Not that Lucas failed to turn me into his zombie love slave, but that Hecate is right, and there's no such thing as magic. It was exciting for a while when we'd all convinced ourselves that our good luck spell was working. The world seemed more colorful, full of previously unimagined possibilities. It was thrilling to think the four of us could wield such power. But if the love spell had worked, I'd know it by now. So that's the end of it, then.

All that's left to worry about is letting Lucas down gently. I hope he's not too upset that I haven't developed any powerful feelings for him overnight.

SUNDAY, NOVEMBER 13, 9:03 A.M.

Okay, this is unsettling. I flipped through the Book of Shadows a minute ago and found a new drawing in it—some kind of floating creature, but with a long head and beak. Where did it come from? I know I often go blank while I'm drawing these, but usually I at least realize what I've done right at the end.

I *know* there was nothing like this in the book when I went to bed. And . . . I've been asleep all night. Did I wake up and do it without remembering? Did I do it in my sleep?

It almost feels completely detached from me, like the book generated the picture itself while I was sleeping. But that's definitely not possible.

I know I was anxious last night about the results of our ritual, but this is getting out of hand. I need to find some way to control this compulsion to draw in the book. It's starting to creep me out.

Lara: OMG. Mel, have you heard yet? WHERE R U??? I can't believe this.

Lara: The whole school has been turned completely upside down.

Mel: What are you talking about? I'm running late this morning, I haven't heard anything at all.

Lara: The spell! Lucas's spell! It worked and it has changed EVERYTHING.

Mel: Um . . . no. No it didn't work. I'm pretty sure I'd know, wouldn't I? But I feel exactly the same.

Lara: That's what I mean! I was wrong, Mel. It's not you! Lucas's spell was never about you.

Mel: Oh.

Mel: Ohhhhh.

Mel: So, wait. Who was it about?

Lara: That's the best part. It's Tyler Hoyt!

Mel: WHAT?

Lara: YES

Mel: NO

Lara: YES

Mel: Lara, think about what you're saying. Are we talking about the same person? Tyler Hoyt, the super jock, super popular, super Christian captain of the football team?

Lara: You forgot SUPER STRAIGHT.

Mel: No shit! So . . . what the hell is going on??? No, forget it. We need to have this conversation in person. I need to see for myself.

MONDAY, NOVEMBER 14, 5:26 P.M.

Oh my God, what a day! And to think, last night I thought the most exciting thing that could come out of that ritual was me developing new feelings for Lucas. But that's nothing to the shit storm Lucas actually created. I couldn't believe it all when Lara told me—I had to see for myself. But apparently it's all true! Lucas and Tyler are now . . . an item? It's completely unexpected! I never even knew Lucas was gay. I mean, *obviously*, since I let Lara convince me that he was totally into me. I can't even express how relieved I feel to know that he isn't, and his romantic interest is pointed in another direction completely.

So I'm still kind of piecing together what happened exactly, but we all cornered him at lunch today and he gave us most of the story.

It turns out that the name Lucas focused on during our ritual was not mine, but Tyler Hoyt's. His original plan was to wait until Monday to try to talk to Tyler and see what happened. Since he wasn't expecting any change, there didn't seem any reason to rush. But performing the ritual changed his mind—the intensity of the energy in the room made him eager to see what effects the spell had produced as soon as possible. And when he woke up Saturday morning, the strangest thing had happened: the bulb from the spell had bloomed!

Which is extremely bizarre. I mean, it was a *bulb*. Those things are supposed to sit in the ground for months before they finally produce some green shoots, and then it's even more time before they grow to full size and bud and bloom. But Lucas says he woke up that morning to find a purplish black tulip fully grown in the jar we set out. He said at first he was convinced someone must have come in his room and replaced it, but who would do that? And when he checked the bottom, the name was still carved in the bulb, the way he had left it the night before.

On an impulse, he headed over to the football field where he knew Tyler would be having Saturday practice. He watched from the sidelines, and when it was over he approached Tyler and said, "Nice job."

Tyler thanked him, and Lucas, feeling brave, said, "You looked good out there."

"What do you mean?" said Tyler. "Do you mean, 'you' as in the team?"

"Well, yeah," said Lucas. "The team looked good. And you. You specifically. You looked good."

At that point, Lucas was starting to worry he'd gone too far. It could be dangerous, making an obvious pass at one of the biggest homophobes in school. He was preparing to run as fast as he could in case Tyler called on all his football buddies to kick Lucas's ass. But instead Tyler smiled and looked really flattered. So then Lucas became even bolder and asked him what he was doing after practice, and if he wanted to go grab some food or something.

The upshot was, they wound up spending the whole day together and having a really good time, and they went back to Lucas's to play video games and TYLER HOYT WANTED TO MAKE OUT WITH HIM. It's perfectly surreal to even *think* about such a thing, if you know Tyler at all.

Lucas didn't do it, though. He told Tyler he wanted to wait until they knew each other better, but really he was disturbed by the fact that we planted this idea in Tyler's head. He said it didn't feel right—almost like taking advantage of someone while they're drunk.

Tyler was disappointed, but he said he understood. Luckily for Lucas, Tyler found it sweet that Lucas wants to take things slow.

I don't know how well this will work over the long term, but I'm glad Lucas is at least trying to set some boundaries.

On Sunday they texted a bit, but Lucas was still feeling like the whole thing was a dream and he was going to wake up from it at any minute. Or at least, once they were back on school on Monday, Tyler would obviously pretend nothing had happened and act as if he didn't even know Lucas's name. I mean, that was probably the best case scenario—that's how these things work, right? And Lucas was prepared for that.

But that's when the most astounding thing of all happened! Because Lucas came into school being chill and acting the same as ever, and he was studying in the cafeteria before class like he always does. And he sort of sees Tyler across the cafeteria with a bunch of his football jock buddies, but he doesn't even look over or try to make eye contact, because he doesn't want to make anything excessively awkward. And the next thing he knows, Tyler comes right up to him, and then—right in front of everyone!—Tyler straight up asks him to be his date to the Winter Formal.

WHAAAAAAT. Like, this is completely unprecedented. Inconceivable, even. Sure, I've seen news stories about same sex couples going to school dances and it being no big deal, but not at *this* school. No way.

Not with the mega-church running this whole place everything from the students to the teachers and administration to the PTA. And Tyler—he's deeply embedded in this system and has been his whole life. If anyone knows the consequences of making this kind of public declaration, it's him. So how could he? And what will happen now?

Oh, I suppose I should mention that Lucas said yes. Which is thrilling and terrifying all at the same time, even for me as his friend. But he said he didn't know what else to do, with all those people around, watching. He didn't want to humiliate Tyler, especially since he was the one who got him into this situation.

Every time I catch a glimpse of Lucas, he looks like someone in a state of shock. I have to admit, I'm a little worried about him. The teasing Lara and I have endured over supposedly being lesbians is one thing, but it's manageable. But what Lucas is facing now . . . He's *so* visible, and doing so much to confront people on their most basic assumptions and prejudices. I can't help thinking that sounds dangerous. Once the shock has worn off, who knows what people will do? There could be some serious harassment, or worse. It's all very exciting now, but what happens if things turn . . . violent?

It's not only that. I'm concerned about the lasting effects of this spell, and I'm sure Lucas is too. He said he doesn't feel comfortable doing anything physical with Tyler, but how long will he be able to put him off? No one can predict what will happen down the road. The spell might wear off eventually, and what will Tyler think or do when his old self resurfaces? On the other hand, what if the spell never wears off? Lucas and Tyler could be bound together forever. None of us thought about that when we did the spell. We thought we were messing around.

But never mind the future—even the present is beyond anything I could have imagined. Lucas! Tyler! Official public boyfriends! The whole social order of the school, shaken to its foundations! It's all so huge, I can't even process it right now. What a day!

TUESDAY, NOVEMBER 15, 5:16 P.M.

I swear, a part of me woke up this morning wondering whether yesterday's events really happened. I actually read over my last diary entry to reassure myself that I didn't hallucinate it. And even then, I somehow felt that when I got to school, everything would have gone back to normal. I'm not sure how, but I figured maybe Tyler would have told his friends the whole thing was a big joke, and Lucas would fade back into social obscurity, and things would be more or less the way they always were.

But I could not have been more wrong.

It's like living in the End Time out of the Book of Revelation—I don't know how else to describe it. I'm half expecting frogs to come raining down from the sky. The whole school is upside down trying to figure out how to react to this sudden change.

I think it would have been so much easier for everyone if this news had revolved around some random kids who were already outsiders to Middleton High School's social scene. Someone like me, for example. Then everyone could have gone into their prepared techniques of shunning, teasing, harassing, and of course condescendingly "praying for those poor sinners to find their way to Jesus." Totally predictable.

But the thing is, they can't really do that with Tyler, because Tyler is *popular*. Like, really, really popular. And even Lucas isn't exactly an outcast. Even if *I* know he doesn't take it very seriously, technically he is still a member of the mega-church. And because he's funny and outgoing, he's actually pretty well liked, despite hanging around with me and Lara. And now he's the lead in the school play, plus he's been best friends with Caleb for years, which always bought him a lot of social cachet, at least before Caleb started acting out.

Now none of the popular mega-church kids are exactly sure what to do. A few of them fell back on their training/brainwashing and immediately turned on Tyler and Lucas and started accusing them of being agents of the Devil and what have you. But they were definitely in the minority, and they weren't even the most powerful members of the mega-church clique. Plus, some of them have started to weaken in their resolve, now that they see they're not getting much support. As for the rest . . . I can't say anyone's gone out of their way to be directly supportive, or said anything explicitly in defense of gay rights. But Tyler's still getting invited to parties and included in plans, and he still had lunch with the rest of the football jocks yesterday and today. Actually, Lucas has left our table to join him the last two days, and no one from the team has tried to shut him out or drive him away. Everyone's been . . .

basically friendly! It's kind of incredible. I never thought I'd see something like this at our school.

Of course, that's on the student side. As for the adults, it's a different story. It didn't take long for news to get around about Tyler asking Lucas to the dance, and even though nothing formal has happened, rumor has it the administration is already scrambling, trying to figure out what to do about the issue. Part of the problem is that it wouldn't be the first time people brought same-sex dates to a school dance. There's no official rule against it, so sometimes people go with friends if they don't have a date. No one has ever batted an eyelash at that. Everyone acknowledges that this situation is different, but no one knows quite how to deal with it. And from what I hear, the great gears of the mega-church itself are starting to churn as it turns its attention to this problem. I have no idea what will happen then.

I've been talking the whole thing through incessantly with Lara and Caleb, but I kind of wonder what Lucas thinks about it all. Other than him telling us what happened, I've hardly heard from him since this all began. Between his play rehearsals and his new position as boyfriend to the most popular jock in school, we haven't seen much of him. What must it be like to be on the inside of all this? I can't imagine how that feels . . . coming out of the closet so publicly and suddenly.

Maybe I'll check in with him and see how he's doing.

E-MAIL TRANSCRIPT

From: Melanie V.
To: Lucas P.
Date: Tuesday, November 15, at 5:30 P.M.
Subject: You okay?

Hey, Lucas. Um . . . not to pry or anything but just checking in. I wanted to see how you were doing. You've been a little busy lately! ;) Understatement of the century, haha.

I don't know, from what I see and hear from a distance, everything seems to be going great. I wanted to hear about it directly from you, I guess. How are you dealing with all the attention? And how are things with Tyler?

We can talk any time. Let me know.

From: Lucas P.
To: Melanie V.
Date: Tuesday, November 15, at 5:38 P.M.
Subject: RE: You okay?

Heeeeey, Mel. Thanks for checking in. I feel like I've been in a daze this past week. It's like I'm watching some outrageous reality TV show, only it's my real life.

I'd love to talk about it, but I'm not sure what to say. Things with Tyler are . . . good? Really good. Considering we didn't even know each other before, I'm amazed at how well we get along. I worried that it would be awkward hanging out with him, but whenever we're together, we seem to click.

His friends have been very accepting too. I was petrified at first that all those football guys were going to beat the crap out of me, or Tyler, or both of us. But it hasn't been like that at all—everyone's been perfectly chill and welcoming. Maybe there have been one or two off-color jokes or insulting terms, but they always apologize when they screw up, and I can tell they mean well.

The adults are a different story. My parents have been supportive, luckily, but Tyler's parents and the rest of the mega-church hierarchy . . . not so much. Still, even that has its silver lining. Tyler and I have had some really powerful conversations about his relationship with his parents, and what it was like growing up in the church, and how controlled and manipulated he always felt. As difficult as it's been for him, he's really positive about using his own struggles to help other kids dealing with similar situations.

I really like him, Mel. I mean, I always thought he was attractive, but he seemed like a massive jerk in every other way. But the more I get to know him, the more it seems like that was a screen for who he really is—compassionate, determined, inspiring. It seems like this whole whirlwind experience has brought out the best in him.

From: Melanie V.
To: Lucas P.
Date: Tuesday, November 15, at 5:40 P.M.
Subject: RE: You okay?

That sounds wonderful. But do you ever worry about . . . you know. The fact that the whole thing started as a spell?

From: Lucas P.
To: Melanie V.
Date: Tuesday, November 15, at 6:27 P.M.
Subject: RE: You okay?

Of course I do. I think about it all the time. But I don't know what to do about it, or if there's anything I can do. Everything about this relationship feels so right, but at the same time, there's a shadow over it. Because I have no way to tell if any of it is real. Lately I don't even know what "real" means.

I swear, Mel, I would never have done that spell if I'd thought it would work. After the luck spell, I had wondered a little of the magic we did might be real, but Hecate convinced me it definitely wasn't. I meant what I said that day, about doing it as an experiment. All I wanted was to prove to myself and you guys that Hecate was right.

So I picked the most ridiculous, impossible, utterly out-of-my-league person I could think of, and figured, why not? It's not going to work anyway. Why not give myself twenty-four hours of enjoying the fantasy? Then, when it all turns out to be make-believe, I can have a nice laugh about it and no harm done.

Picking Tyler seemed like the best possible test of our abilities. But also safe. Because I really couldn't imagine any situation in which he would speak to me. I was positive the spell wouldn't work. I figured, once we did it, I'd be able to relax about everything else—the good luck, the role in the play, the rituals. I could go back to thinking it was silly fun, and not worry about disturbing the universe.

Only, that's not what happened.

As soon as I realized the spell worked, I felt awful about it. I never wanted my first boyfriend to be the result of a trick, and I'd give anything to take it back now.

But at the same time, everything Tyler says to me seems so genuine and sincere—he doesn't seem mind-controlled or entranced. If anything, he seems liberated.

I don't know what to think, Mel. I lie awake at night, wondering if I broke him or saved him. He seems happy now, and he says he was miserable before. Can I trust that? Talking to Tyler now, it's hard for me to believe he could ever be happy under the control of the mega-church, so maybe this really was for the best. Or maybe I want to believe that, because it lets me off the hook.

All I know is, it feels really good to be out of the closet and open about who I am. And it feels great to have a partner standing by my side, supporting me and going through the same things. I only wish I had gotten here by a more honest path.

WEDNESDAY, NOVEMBER 16, 5:03 P.M.

Even after talking to Lucas, I still can't believe what's been going on at school. Things are so different there lately! It's mostly good, but every day I feel like I'm waiting for the other shoe to drop.

At least I have my drawings as an outlet for all this extra anxiety. I've given up on the idea of trying to stop drawing. I think that was normal nervousness about trying anything new, but I realize now, these drawings are nothing to be frightened of—they're good for me. Drawing in the Book of Shadows is the only thing that calms me down lately. I always feel so much better after I've done one. I don't know what I'd do if I didn't have this outlet.

It's so soothing that I'm often not aware I've conjured up another one until a bell rings or my mom calls me. Only then do I realize I have my pen in my hand and a drawing in front of me. It's like being startled out of a trance, almost. But it's a really pleasant feeling, to get away from all the usual noise going on in my brain.

I don't know, there's probably something abnormal about that, but I've kind of stopped fighting it because it feels so therapeutic. The feeling of blankness I have while I'm drawing is a bit disconcerting, but afterward I always feel relaxed, calm, and especially powerful. Like nothing can bother me.

I haven't stopped seeing the gruesome, creeping creatures out of the corner of my eye, but it doesn't bother me as much as it used to. I can see them better now. . . . I've figured out that if I let my eyes relax and concentrate a bit, sometimes I can make out their shapes and their expressions. And that makes them less scary. One I saw today was a lizard with skin like a rock. He was almost cute, despite the fangs.

I'm not sure if they're real or in my head, but I don't think they mean me any harm. Anyway, it's kind of cool that no one else can see them—like having my own little secret.

The whole Lucas/Tyler situation isn't playing out at all as I would have expected.

I had been worried that they would face some serious threats from the Bible thumpers in our class. That they were putting themselves in real danger. But not only has that not happened, somehow Lucas and Tyler have wound up as the school's celebrity power couple?? They're all anyone talks about these days, and from what I can tell from my lowly position on the social scale, most of the chatter is positive. More and more people are really excited about the idea of them going to the Winter Formal together. I even saw someone circulating a petition to the administration to make them formally accept same sex couples at school functions. I can't even describe how unimaginable this would have been a month ago. And of course,

I'm all too aware that if it were two obscure geeks who were making this statement, they wouldn't be getting any support at all, and would probably be dealing with some scary shit. But I guess Lucas wasn't so dumb in setting his sights on Tyler Hoyt. It turns out popularity like that comes with some serious social benefits, and people have been more willing to change their attitude on gay rights than they are to turn their back on one of the school's most popular kids and most valued athletes.

So now, with the support of most of the student body, Lucas and Tyler have become accidental activists for this cause. It's a bit surprising because I can't remember Lucas ever taking an interest in anything political or relating to school policy before. His attitude has always been to fly below the radar and not cause too many waves. And for Tyler it's even more outlandish! I mean, I think he was dating Jessa Maxwell only like a month and a half ago? And he was far more likely to rough up some kid for being a "homo" than to take a stand for gay rights.

As for me, all I can really do is sit back and watch the fireworks. It's like a new day is dawning at Middleton High School.

WEDNESDAY, NOVEMBER 23, 5:49 P.M.

This conversation I had with Lara and Caleb has got me think-ing. Or really it was a debate between the two of them, because at the time I didn't have much to add. But it gave me a lot to chew over.

We were hanging out as usual in Lucas's basement, though he was off at rehearsal, or maybe with Tyler. He's hard to keep track of these days. Anyway, we were dissecting the week's events for the zillionth time, and the sense of surreality we've all experienced since performing the love spell. It seems like it's all given Caleb a completely new perspective on magic. Originally he presented himself as this big skeptic, who didn't believe in anything supernatural. Then he seemed to be nervous that some of it might be real. But everything that has happened since our last spell has apparently cured him of his trepidation. He had a kind of fire in his eyes this afternoon as he was talking about what an incredible success the spell has been.

It shook me for a moment to hear Caleb describe the spell as a success. In my conversations with Lucas, we focused more on the negative consequences of the spell, and the possible damage it might do in the long run. But Caleb isn't wrong—the spell was a success. At least in the sense that it proved we really can do magic. I've been too distracted lately to give much thought to that.

Caleb, however, has apparently been fixating on the larger implications of our spell work. According to him, now that we have this proof of our magical ability, we need to learn more about this power and how best to wield it. If these spells can be used to control other people, think of what we might be able to do. Caleb had all kinds of hypotheses he wanted to experiment with, like how far away you could influence people, and how many at a time, and what kinds of things you could make them do.

Lara, though—she had a different view. She said that we were getting into a dangerous game. Then she started talking about the dangers associated with practicing black magic.

Black magic! That seems like an extreme description of what happened.

I understand where she's coming from. I was squeamish about this spell from the beginning. And Lucas agrees that the ethics of it were a bit shady. But it's not *evil*. From Lara's own description, black magic involves causing harm to other people or tapping into evil forces. Clearly that means cursing people or putting them in danger—things like that. Helping two people fall in love is totally different.

Yes, maybe it was a bad idea to mess around with this kind of spell, not knowing what it would do. But based on Lucas's descriptions and everything I've seen, the spell has produced nothing but good effects. Lucas is happy, Tyler is happy. The whole school has become more open-minded and accepting. Even the administrators are being forced to reconsider decades of unfair, discriminatory policies. That doesn't sound like black magic to me.

Lara disagreed, though. She kept going on about tampering with free will—as if Tyler is little more than a zombie being controlled by our whims. I see her point, except Tyler isn't acting like a zombie. He's still going to his classes and his practices, and other than this one thing, he isn't behaving in any particularly unusual way. Plus, he's become even more of an activist for LGBTQ rights than Lucas—he's been leading the charge the whole way. He's been lobbying the administration for an official change to the school dance rules, and also working with the dance committee to donate money from the dance to gay charities. No one would ever have dared suggest anything like that here, even two weeks ago—and all that has been on his own initiative, not because anyone was making him do it.

But Lara persisted—she said the changes in Tyler's personality were unnatural. We all know that the Tyler of two weeks ago wouldn't have dreamed of doing any of this. So where is it coming from?

Caleb argued that it had to have been in Tyler somewhere, even if we didn't see it. At most, we activated something that had been latent in him all along. But Lara said we had no evidence of that, and it was a blatantly self-serving position. Plus, it was inconsistent with what Caleb had been saying earlier, about how much power we have. If we really have this kind of power, we need to be extra careful of how we wield it.

Now I'm not sure what to believe. I love the changes I've seen at Middleton High recently. Maybe because Lara is in a heterosexual relationship, it's harder for her to see how much Lucas and Tyler's activism has meant to oppressed minorities at this school. She dismisses the good they've done, because it's not important to her.

But on the other hand, I think about Tyler, and his position. He's happy with Lucas, yeah—but I've also heard that he's been living with an aunt since his father threw him out of the house. And he's had to stop going to all his social activities, since they're all church run. Plus he's having problems with the football coach, who of course is another member of the mega-church. Would Tyler really have freely chosen all that? And if not, what responsibility do we all bear for putting him in that situation?

In the end, how do any of us know what we want? What does it even mean to freely choose something? We're all a constellation of influences. The spell clearly had an effect on Tyler, but so did a lifetime growing up in that oppressive church. How is our influence any worse than theirs?

TUESDAY, NOVEMBER 29, 4:29 P.M.

Everything is such a mess, lately. I wonder if Lucas was really the glue holding our little group together all along. Lately he's been spending more time with Tyler, working on their activist projects. He's become such a big deal at school, we hardly see him anymore, and the balance has shifted in our group. Lara and Caleb are always snapping at each other, which normally I'd love to blame Caleb for, except Lara's been testy with me, too, and I don't even know why.

The other day, we were hanging out at Lucas's, waiting for him to come home from rehearsal, and Lara and Caleb were arguing again over the moral implications of the magic we've done, and listening to them was really stressing me out and getting on my nerves, so I tried to shut it out. The next thing I knew,

Lara was shaking me by the shoulder and saying my name. "Mel, what the hell are you doing?"

I kind of came back into myself and realized I'd taken out the Book of Shadows and was drawing in it again. And I guess Lara had never seen my drawings before. I don't think I've ever deliberately tried to hide them from her or anyone else. But except for Lucas seeing it that one time, I've been keeping them private. I do feel bad because I used to share *everything* with Lara—I could hardly imagine having a thought I didn't tell her about. But this felt more natural to keep to myself.

Anyway, when she saw them she kind of flipped out. She said they were disturbing and nightmarish, which . . . well, I suppose they are, in all honesty. But I've come to think they are sort of interesting-looking, too—beautiful in a unique sort of way. Lara didn't agree. She kept asking where my ideas came from, and I told her I didn't know, but that sometimes I get inspired. Isn't that how all art happens?

Maybe that was a little disingenuous. It does seem likely that my drawings have something to do with all our magical explorations. But is that a bad thing? Lara was trying to make it sound like some malevolent force was planting these images in my head, but that's not how I see it. It's all the energy we released during our rituals—I think it opened up some creative corners of my mind and helped me access material that was there all along. I tried to explain this to Lara, but she wouldn't listen.

Finally Lucas walked in and figured out what we were talking about. He defended my drawings to Lara, saying he thought they showed a lot of talent. He compared my newfound talent to Tyler's awakening thanks to the love spell. Lucas has become convinced that the ritual we performed couldn't have caused a fundamental change in Tyler, but merely released something that was already inside him. Something similar must be taking place with my drawing ability.

But Lara wouldn't accept any of our explanations. She said we were making excuses, and that book was taking over our minds.

That pissed me right off. It's like she doesn't think I'm capable of making something creative, unless it's with some kind of supernatural help. Like she thinks I'm completely worthless without the book. Which is so shitty and unfair.

And the more she tried to convince me, the angrier I became. I was so furious, all my annoyances with her over the past couple of weeks bubbled up. I got up in Lara's face and started yelling at her, all about how she was jealous of my talent and that maybe she wasn't the only cool and accomplished one anymore. And it killed her that I might have my own skill that she didn't know anything about, and she would do anything to take that away from me. That she was trying to undermine me because she likes me dependent on her, the way I always have been, her little sidekick who has to hang out with her friends and go where she wants because I don't have any kind of life of my own.

And there was this moment, in the middle of my tirade, when I looked into her face and . . . and I was still screaming at her, but it was like a part of me was calm and standing outside myself, looking at what I was doing to her. And I could see that she was afraid of me. That she was afraid I was going to hit her.

I've never seen that look on her face before. It was the worst feeling. How could she think that about me? How could my best friend be afraid of me?

But then I realized, how could she not? That's who I am. She's seen me lose control with people before. Why shouldn't she be scared?

I've only ever started fights with assholes and idiots before. I'd never do that to a friend. But how could she be sure of that? How can *I* be sure of that?

When that realization hit me, it was almost as if I was the one who'd been punched. I took a step back, reeling from the situation. I was scared for Lara too, because in that moment, I really didn't know what I was capable of.

I didn't trust myself, with how angry I was right then, so I grabbed the book and went home and turned off my phone because I didn't want to hear anything more from her, or from any of them.

Mel: I'm sorry.

Mel: God, Lara, I'm so sorry for how I lost it back there. You didn't deserve that.

Mel: I totally understand if you never want to speak to me again. I hate that I did that to you, but I understand if you can't forgive me.

Mel: Okay. That's all I have to say. I'm sorry.

Lara: Hey. Are you okay?

Mel: Am I okay? OMG, Lara, how are you even asking that. You're so sweet, but I'm the one who should be asking about you. Only I'm scared to ask.

Lara: It's okay. I'm fine.

Lara: I mean, I've had better afternoons. But mostly I'm worried about you.

Mel: Why are you worrying about me?

Lara: You're my friend. And I don't think you're doing very well right now.

Mel: No. I'm awful.

Lara: You're not awful. You're not an awful person, okay?

Mel: Okay.

Lara: But there's stuff going on that we need to deal with.

Mel: Yeah. I know.

Lara: Thanks for the apology.

Lara: I'm sorry too, for what it's worth.

Lara: I didn't mean to act like you aren't talented. That was shitty of me to say.

Mel: It's fine. I overreacted.

Mel: It's just . . . I don't know. Those drawings are really important to me for some reason. It's something I'm good at, something I care about, that's only for me. I've never really had anything like that before.

Mel: But it's okay if you don't like them.

Lara: No, I do. I think they're beautiful, in fact . . . in a dark kind of way. I didn't mean to say they weren't.

Lara: Will you make one for me?

Mel: I don't know . . . I'd love to, but I don't want to tear another page out of the book.

Mel: I'm sorry. Guess I've kind of become superstitious about it.

Lara: That's okay, it doesn't have to come from the book. Do one on a random sheet of notebook paper or whatever.

Mel: Um . . . sure. I can do that. Why not? I'd love to. I'll make something special for you.

TUESDAY, NOVEMBER 29, 4:55 P.M.

God, what is wrong with me? I promised Lara a special drawing, and now I can't do it! It really meant a lot to me that she asked for one. She's one of the few people in the world whose opinion really matters to me, and it was upsetting to think she didn't appreciate my newfound talent. So for her to ask for one . . . I don't know if she really meant it or if she was trying to be nice and make up for our fight, but either way, I appreciated the gesture.

But now I'm sitting here with a notebook on my lap surrounded by balled up pieces of paper because everything I draw looks . . . ugly and amateurish. I don't understand it! Normally I don't have to think about my drawings at all. I pull out my book, put a pen in my hand, and go on autopilot. And when I snap to, there's some cool-looking demon thing in front of me. But now . . . I don't know. I try to make my hand do what it usually does, but I get nothing but worthless scribbles or cutesy doodles. Nothing like my usual style.

I don't know what I'm going to tell Lara. I really wanted to do this for her, but for some reason I can't seem to produce anything but junk.

And the worst part is, I know Lara is going to use this as evidence that she was right all along, and the Book of Shadows really is responsible for all my drawings. But it's not true! I don't believe it.

I don't want to believe it.

l which made a lot of sense to me. And I think Lara was

g to relent too, and I was relieved and ready to put this all

d me.

it then Caleb suggested another experiment. He said if I

wanted to prove that I can control the drawings, I could

draw one with my eyes closed, or wearing a blindfold. If

ent, I shouldn't be able to do it with my eyes closed, and

book is enchanting my drawings, then it shouldn't matter

looking at what I'm doing or not.

ot a chance, I told him. There's no way I'm going to scribble

r my beautiful book to prove a point.

f course, now part of me is worried that it's true, and all

drawings I've done are really examples of some kind of

al mind control. But that can't be it . . . can it? The magic

done wasn't created by the book; the Book of Shadows

ning but a tool. The magical energy and intention comes

ts users.

hink Caleb was kind of annoyed that I vetoed his plan, but

y book. I don't have to submit to his stupid experiment if

t want to.

WEDNESDAY, NOVEMBER 30, 5

I saw Lara today. And I had to tell her what
drawings. I even showed her a couple of m
could see I wasn't making it up to get ou
course she did what I expected, and took i
and ominous way possible.

She said, "So it only works when the bc

Which was infuriating, because once
ing that I don't have any talent on my ow
I could make something special is throu;
magic force. At least Lucas stood up for
necessarily mean anything so sinister. May
mood, or maybe I don't work well unde
duce for someone else. Creativity is like
always turn it on when you want to.

All which made a lot of sense to me. And I think Lara was starting to relent too, and I was relieved and ready to put this all behind me.

But then Caleb suggested another experiment. He said if I really wanted to prove that I can control the drawings, I could try to draw one with my eyes closed, or wearing a blindfold. If it's talent, I shouldn't be able to do it with my eyes closed, and if the book is enchanting my drawings, then it shouldn't matter if I'm looking at what I'm doing or not.

Not a chance, I told him. There's no way I'm going to scribble all over my beautiful book to prove a point.

Of course, now part of me is worried that it's true, and all these drawings I've done are really examples of some kind of magical mind control. But that can't be it . . . can it? The magic we've done wasn't created by the book; the Book of Shadows is nothing but a tool. The magical energy and intention comes from its users.

I think Caleb was kind of annoyed that I vetoed his plan, but it is *my* book. I don't have to submit to his stupid experiment if I don't want to.

WEDNESDAY, NOVEMBER 30, 5:22 P.M.

I saw Lara today. And I had to tell her what happened with the drawings. I even showed her a couple of my false starts, so she could see I wasn't making it up to get out of doing it. But of course she did what I expected, and took it in the most gloomy and ominous way possible.

She said, "So it only works when the book is involved, then?"

Which was infuriating, because once again she was implying that I don't have any talent on my own. That the only way I could make something special is through some kind of dark magic force. At least Lucas stood up for me. He said it didn't necessarily mean anything so sinister. Maybe I wasn't in the right mood, or maybe I don't work well under the pressure to produce for someone else. Creativity is like that, right? You can't always turn it on when you want to.

SATURDAY, DECEMBER 3, 11:27 A.M.

I feel sick. I should never have let Caleb get away with his dumb trick! Although . . . maybe it's better to know what I know now? Except I'm still not even sure exactly what happened.

It was Friday night and Lucas had managed to get his hands on a bottle of rum. We were mixing that with juice, and I think we all got a little tipsier than we meant to. Anyway, we were sitting around watching movies and playing video games, and without really thinking about it, I pulled my book out and started drawing in it. And I was so intent on the drawing that I wasn't paying much attention to what was going on around me. But the next thing I knew, Caleb was flicking off the lights so the only light in the room was from a couple of candles. I kept drawing, and after a couple of minutes, he blew those out too. But I barely registered it. Somehow my hand knew where to go, even in total darkness.

I didn't think about it at the time, but I realize now he was trying to trick me into doing his "experiment." He didn't like that I refused him before, so he found a sneaky way to get me to do it. And I fell for it, like an idiot.

I was dimly aware of the others sitting around me, still giggling a bit from the alcohol. After a while Lucas asked if he could have a go. I don't know why I let him—normally I never would. But thanks to the liquor in my system, I didn't even think about it. I handed it to him with the pen. He drew for a while, but I could tell he wasn't taking it seriously—he kept giggling as he drew and saying, "Whoops!"

Then he passed it to Caleb, and on to Lara, until we had all given it a try. At some point I think Lucas turned it into a kind of drinking game? Like you had to take another drink every time your pen went off the page or whatever. So by the end we were all *really* drunk. And I don't even remember half of what happened.

Eventually we all passed out on the couch or the floor without even turning the lights back on. At least, as far as I can tell. All I really know is that I woke up in the morning with my head pounding, empty cups everywhere, and the book lying on the floor in front of me. And suddenly it all came back to me and I felt even worse, thinking how could I have let everyone scribble all over my precious book all night? It had to be completely ruined now.

But Caleb, who had woken up before me, said, "Why don't you open it and see what we did." Hesitantly I flipped it open. And there were all these new drawings.

Not scribbles at all. Real drawings of unearthly creatures, like the ones I've been doing all along. Only they were even scarier and more violent-looking than the others. Especially one of a giant horned beast with a huge, gaping mouth and teeth like long, thick needles. Even though I've become accustomed to the style of these drawings now, that one made even *me* a little jumpy. It looked like it was ready to crawl off the page and devour me.

And while I distinctly remembered us all letting the pen run off the page, I couldn't find any places in the drawings where that happened.

At that point, fear descended on me as a bone-chilling calm. How could it be possible to produce drawings like that—all four of us—without even looking? I told myself before that the book was nothing more than a tool to help us create the magic we chose. But maybe a part of me knew the truth all along, even though I didn't want to admit it. We thought we were directing the magic to suit our own purposes. But all this time, it's been the book directing us.

SATURDAY, DECEMBER 3, 6:37 P.M.

Now that everyone has sobered up, it seems I'm not the only one a bit dismayed by what happened last night. I don't think anyone can deny anymore that the book has power—serious power. And that somehow it's been exerting that power over us.

I was over at Lucas's earlier, talking with the others about what this means, what we should do. Caleb still maintains that everything the book has done so far has been good. Which is arguably true, but there's something about it that makes me nervous all the same. Maybe the creepiness of the drawings, and the bad dreams they sometimes give me. I'm not the only one, either. Though Lara who was so excited about the book when we started, before growing more and more nervous about it, is borderline terrified now, worrying that it's leading us down a path toward black magic.

Lucas didn't want to hear that, though. He was offended that anything about his relationship with Tyler might be referred to as "black magic." I know he was initially worried about the questionable morality of love spells, but now that he and Tyler are the most popular couple on campus, he seems to have conveniently forgotten about all that. Lara kept pressing her point, though, and it got me thinking about what happened with Hecate's parents. What if they really were performing black magic without knowing it, and it came back and hurt them in the end?

Finally Caleb said we were arguing in circles, and we weren't going to come to any conclusion without more information about the book. And the only way we could learn more about the book is by talking to Hecate again.

I don't know about this plan. Last time we talked to her, she seemed so sure that all magic was make-believe, and that the book was nothing more than an inert object, with no special powers. Why would she change her position?

But I can't think of any other way to dig up more of the book's history, so we don't have much choice.

SUNDAY, DECEMBER 4, 6:37 P.M.

We went back to Hecate today. As I predicted, she wasn't exactly thrilled to see us, especially since this time we showed up unannounced instead of calling ahead. That was Caleb's idea—he didn't want to give her a chance to refuse us before she even heard our story.

She did try to get us to leave, saying she was busy and had nothing more to say to us on the subject of magic. But Caleb was insistent—he did that thing where he shifts his voice and his whole body and becomes so intense that people do whatever he wants. And Hecate was no exception. She let us in, but she still seemed annoyed. She pointed out that she had already told us to stay away from all this "witchcraft nonsense." Lara was outraged at that, of course. She said it wasn't nonsense, and started telling Hecate all about the drawings in the book. Hecate wasn't impressed, though. She obviously didn't see anything inherently magical about a bunch of kids doodling in a book. I could see Lara was getting frustrated, and finally she told me to get out the book and show it to Hecate.

I didn't see why this would convince her, if nothing else had, but I was wrong. I pulled out the book and opened it up to some of the drawings, and Hecate, who had been kind of rolling her eyes at the whole story, immediately pulled the book over to her and started flipping wildly through it.

"I don't understand," she kept saying. "How did you do this? How did you change this book?"

I had no idea what she was talking about, so finally she asked me if the book was blank when I got it. I told her it was, and she said it didn't used to be. This book was the jewel of her father's collection, his most prized possession. He let her look at it a few times when she was a kid, and she remembers that every page was covered in writing. In all kinds of languages, many different handwritings and where did it all go?

She seemed stunned by what she had seen, and none of us were able to explain it. At last Caleb asked her if she knew anyone who might be able to tell us more, and she nodded.

"The coven," she said. "The other witches my parents used to associate with. Some of them are still in town."

She promised she'd try to track them down for us.

TUESDAY, DECEMBER 6, 6:37 P.M.

I heard from Caleb—Hecate came through for us! She got in touch with some of her parents' old friends and asked them if she could introduce us to them. They were hesitant at first—they've had some bad run-ins with the mega-church during the past few years, and now they've pretty much gone underground. But she found out that the coven is meeting this week, and she gave Caleb an address right outside of town.

It's hard to believe . . . I've been thinking of Hecate's parents and their coven as ancient history. But of course people who were into witchcraft in the sixties and seventies are still around today. Real witches! I wonder what it will be like.

SATURDAY, DECEMBER 10, 1:10 A.M.

I am rapidly coming to the conclusion that Lara is right: everything Hollywood has ever taught me about witches has been wrong.

I should know better by now, but even after the disappointment of meeting Hecate, a part of me still believed that the coven would consist of a bunch of old crones in long black robes, standing around some churning cauldron. Well, actually . . . now that I think about it, that isn't completely false. It just wasn't quite the way I had pictured.

The witches *were* pretty old, but more in the "fat and balding" way than bent, wrinkled, and toothless. It was four women and two men. A couple of women wore long dresses that might pass for robes if you squinted, but the rest were wearing regular clothes. Or well . . . one of the men—Greg, I think?—was wearing sweatpants, sandals, and a Hawaiian shirt, so I don't know if that counts as normal, but it didn't feel very witchy.

And as for the cauldron, they did have a big pot of vegan chili. Not quite the same effect.

The meeting was held in Greg's backyard, where a bunch of kitchen chairs had been set up around a small fire. Hecate introduced us, but at first the witches seemed more interested in her than us. They spent a long time reminiscing about how they remembered her as a little girl. Other topics of conversation included property values, techniques for weatherproofing, and the latest activities of the mega-church. In other words, in was intensely dull.

After a while I noticed Lucas nudging Caleb, and I was pretty sure I could read his mind. *What are we doing at this lame old-people party?* I was ready to leave whenever they gave the word, but Caleb didn't forget why we had come. He waited for a lull in the conversation, then he reached for my bag and pulled out the Book of Shadows, asking if anyone knew anything about it.

From the heavy silence that followed, you could tell that they recognized it immediately. Greg started to reach for the book, but Caleb pulled it back into his arms, and asked him again to tell us what he knew.

A woman named Leora was the one who gave us most of the story, though. She spoke up first, saying she'd been sick of the book before she ever even laid eyes on it. Then she told us about Bob and Rosemary, Hecate's parents.

Bob learned of the book's existence sometime in the mid 1970s. He was in contact with all these rare book dealers specializing in esoteric texts, and one of them told him about this book. It was in Austria at the time. The dealer claimed it was the most powerful grimoire to escape the fires of the Inquisition, and that was thanks to some very dark magic. Leora said any sensible witch would have viewed that description as a warning, but Bob and Rosemary were overconfident in their powers, and they lusted after that book like nothing else. They started talking about it nonstop, at every meeting, trying to convince the others that it was going to revolutionize their magical practice.

Bob wrote to the owner inquiring about buying it, or maybe trading some of the books already in his library for it, but the owner wasn't interested in selling—not for any price. That fact alone was enough to convince Bob this book was the real deal. So he changed his tune—he asked the guy if he could visit and look at it. Study it for a couple of weeks. The guy said no, but Bob wouldn't accept that. He kept writing and writing, and he and Rosemary pressured the rest of the coven to perform spells to act on the man's will.

At last he received the answer he wanted. Or at least that's what he told them. All Leora could say for sure was that Bob left for Austria one day, leaving Rosemary at home with little Hecate. And when he came back a few weeks later, he had the book. He said the man had had a change of heart and decided to sell it after all, but it was all very mysterious. Leora seemed pretty suspicious of what methods Bob might have used to get the book away from the man.

After that, they tried to incorporate the book into the coven's ritual practice, but some of the other witches were nervous about it. An object with that kind of magical power would pick up on the energy around it. Even if the book wasn't evil in itself, it could become that way by being acquired through malevolent means. It turned into a big fight between the witches who sided with Bob and Rosemary and wanted to use the book, and those who wanted nothing to do with it. The coven lost a few members and almost broke up over it, but eventually Bob and Rosemary decided the question by withdrawing from the group themselves. Apparently they decided that whatever powers the book was able to grant them, they weren't interested in sharing them with the rest of the coven.

They moved to a place way out in the country after that, and the others lost track of them. The next thing they heard, Bob had died.

Rosemary came back to the coven after that. She told them she and Bob had been wrong, that they had been irresponsible with the powers they had gained. They had wound up going down a very dark path, though she refused to give specifics. But now she was done with it, and she wanted help.

Leora came to a stop at this point in the story, and looked across the fire at Greg, who shifted a bit in his seat.

"Help with what?" said Lucas.

No one said anything for a minute, until Greg said, "She wanted to get rid of the grimoire. And I offered to help."

"You offered to take it," said Leora. "You wanted to use it yourself."

Greg looked offended. "I would have shared it with everyone. That's where they went wrong, trying to do everything by themselves. They needed the balance provided by a group. We were that group. We could have handled it."

Leora shook her head. "Some of us," she said pointedly, "wanted nothing more to do with the book. We advised Rosemary to destroy it before it could do any more harm. She said she was going to, and I thought that was the end of it. But apparently she couldn't bring herself to. And now it's back."

At this point, Hecate broke in, asking about the old spells. Caleb opened the book and showed everyone all the blank pages, plus the handful of pages we've written or drawn on. Some of the witches gasped or marveled at the change. Then a woman with glasses spoke in a quiet, nervous voice. She said there was a potion. Rosemary had asked for her help with it, and they brewed it together. Once applied to the pages, it was meant to ensure that no one could ever use the book for evil again. When they finished the ritual, the pages were blank. Rosemary had seemed relieved, though she was still nervous enough about it to lock it away in storage and never touch it again for the rest of her life.

"She should have destroyed it," said Leora grimly when the woman with glasses had finished. "There's never any use in doing these things by halves."

That got Greg started again. He started in about how the book is an important artifact of the history of witchcraft, and it would be criminal to destroy it. Bob and Rosemary, he maintained, were headed down a bad path no matter what. The book was a powerful object in the wrong hands, but in the right hands it would have been capable of tremendous good.

"It still would," he said, turning to Caleb. "It belongs with us. The members of this coven have the knowledge and experience to use it properly."

"No," said Leora. "The only safe thing to do is to burn it right now."

She stood up and approached Caleb, her hand outstretched. Greg cried out in protest, and that's when things got messy.

Everyone started talking at once, and everyone had an opinion on what should happen with the book. *My* book.

I had been listening to all their stories with interest, but when they started fighting, it hit me—these witches weren't going to stop at giving us a bit of history. They wanted the book for themselves. Some of them wanted to use it, others wanted to destroy it, but they all agreed that *they* should be in possession of it. Suddenly I felt that same panic I had felt back on that first day, when I had worried about all the other people who might come to claim the book if I didn't grab my chance. The same as that day, a powerful feeling came over me that the book was mine, was meant to be mine. I couldn't let these strangers take it from me.

I watched the argument progress for another minute or two, until I was sure that the witches were completely absorbed in their conflict with one another. Then I made a sign to Caleb, who was still holding my book, and by silent agreement the four of us slipped out and back to our car. Even then, I couldn't relax at all until I was back in my room, the book sitting here on my desk next to me.

Maybe it was wrong of me to try to keep it. Given how I came to possess the book, it's not really any more mine than theirs. But I'm not ready to give it up yet. I'm too attached to it.

Still, the story Leora told did open my eyes. This isn't a toy for us to play with—there is serious magical power in this book. I think probably the wisest choice for now is to put the book away on a shelf in the back of my closet, and not pull it out again until I've learned and studied enough to be able to wield that power without it corrupting me.

TUESDAY, DECEMBER 13, 5:24 P.M.

In all the drama and excitement over the book, I almost forgot there's something else exciting going on—the Winter Formal dance is coming up this week! Wow, I never dreamed I'd write a sentence like that. Historically I am *not* the kind of person who attends boring school dances. That sort of thing is entirely lame in my opinion. But this one is supposed to be totally different, thanks to Lucas and Tyler. I can't believe what miracles they and their friends have performed! All those petitions and everything . . . I didn't believe it would amount to anything except maybe getting them suspended, but they actually achieved their goal! The school board grew nervous about the story getting picked up by the national press and making them look like a bunch of small-minded bigots (which they are). So, hoping to avoid that, they totally caved!

SUNDAY, DECEMBER 11, 2:15 P.M.

Caleb is really annoying me. He keeps trying to get me to take out the book again, or lend it to him. He insists that it's an incredible resource, and it's a waste for us to sit on it instead of studying it and experimenting with it. He even dragged out his "preacher kid" voice and those intense, hypnotizing eyes. But I stood my ground. Maybe some day we'll have the experience and wisdom to make proper use of the Book of Shadows, but after everything we've learned, I'm not taking any chances right now.

Not only is the dance going to let in same sex couples, the whole theme is Over the Rainbow. How cool is that? I figure I'd better go, if for no other reason than to show my support for Lucas and Tyler and other students like them. But I'm also half hoping that it will actually be fun. I don't know, but it feels like . . . a new day dawning for the school, as cheesy as that sounds. Where everyone will be accepted as who they are, instead of forced into these tiny, uncomfortable boxes of social and religious acceptability.

Who knows if that's even possible at a school like ours. But I'm going, and I'm hoping for the best.

FRIDAY, DECEMBER 16, 7:17 P.M.

Back from the dance. Yes, already. It was a fiasco.

I carpooled there with Caleb and Lara (obviously Lucas was going with Tyler), but I had to call my mom to come pick me up. I'm not sure I've ever felt so humiliated in all my life.

When we arrived, I went up to the dance committee table to buy a ticket. Like most people, Caleb and Lara had bought theirs in advance so I told them to go on ahead. I was going to buy one at the door and meet them inside. Well, I asked for a ticket and Betty Fillmore and Madison Lowell were manning the table, and Betty pulled out a ticket and started writing my name on it, and then she said, "Who's your date?"

I told her no one, it was only me. And she looked up all mock apologetic, but I could see the thrill in her eyes as she said,

"I'm sorry, the tickets are only sold as pairs. You need a date if you want to go inside."

"That's ridiculous," I said. "This dance is supposed to be inclusive, and you're shutting me out because I'm here on my own?"

Madison giggled. "Yeah, it's inclusive of gay people. Not losers who can't get dates."

"Why would you even want to go?" added Betty. "What are you going to do during the slow songs, wrap your arms around yourself and sway?" They both cackled like hyenas.

Seriously, fuck them! This has nothing to do with not being able to get a date—I didn't want a date. I don't need one. I'm fine on my own. What the hell is the matter with that?

I was furious, and all I wanted to do was lean across the table and smack the smug looks off their faces. But I didn't! I remembered my talk with Lara, and how I had promised her that I would try harder to control my impulses. I could feel my blood starting to boil, but I took a deep breath and stepped away from the table to get a grip on myself. I kept repeating to myself that they weren't worth it, but after a few minutes I decided to call my mom to take me home, because I didn't know what the hell I might do if I had to look at them again.

So now I'm at home, writing in my journal—like Lara told me to when I have feelings I need to get out. But it's not really helping. I can force myself to be calm, but deep inside, there's a part of me that's still seething. That can't stop thinking of all the terrible things I should have done to them.

How dare they talk to me that way? How dare they treat me like I'm nothing, beneath their contempt, powerless? I'm anything but powerless. Look at what we've done so far! This dance wouldn't even be happening if it weren't for our magic spell. For my Book of Shadows. If Lucas can remake Tyler into a whole new person—if we can turn the whole school into a completely different place . . . what's to stop me from fixing those Queen Bees, too? Or forget fixing them. How about getting rid of them all together? The world is better off without them.

I don't know why I'm even surprised. I had such high hopes for this dance. And not only this dance—this school, this town, maybe even the whole world. Everything has seemed so different lately, so much better. But it's all just surface.

I thought at least I had Lara and the guys for support, but where are they now? Enjoying themselves with their new friends, and none of them have even noticed that I'm missing. They're as bad as the rest of them—they've been using me all this time because they want the power in my Book of Shadows. But it's my book!

Not that I even use it anymore. I wish I could take it out and draw something in it to help me calm down. But I don't dare do that now. I don't trust that book anymore.

I don't know. Does it even matter? Lara told me the book was dangerous, she wanted me to stop using it, so I did. But where did it get me? Lara is at the dance having fun, and I'm still the outcast freak. Lara says violence never solves anything, but being nonviolent doesn't get me much either. I should have gone ahead and ripped that bitch's face off. It wouldn't have made any difference, and it would have felt good. It would have felt *great*.

I'm not as alone as I thought I was. There's someone out there who believes in me.

I tried to go to bed after my last post, but I was too angry and upset to fall asleep, so I lay there, staring out into the darkness of my room. And I started seeing things in the long shadows moving across my walls, but I kept quiet. I didn't want to scare them away this time, the way I usually do when I try to look directly at them. And it worked! The little movements at the corner of my eye gradually became bigger and more deliberate; and if I stayed still and focused, I could see the creatures grinning and making gestures toward me.

At first, they scared me a little, with their pointed teeth and bulbous bodies grasping toward me. I thought they were coming to hurt me or take me away. But eventually I realized they were trying to help me. They were pointing me toward the high shelf in the closet where I'd hidden away the Book of Shadows.

Under their guidance, I crept out of bed and pulled it down. I thought maybe adding another drawing would calm me down and help me get to sleep. But when I opened the book, it flipped to a new page, and there was a spell written on it.

A spell for vengeance.

I didn't write that spell. I didn't write any version of it. And there's no way anyone could have snuck in and written it without my knowing. But there it was, plain as day.

It's the Book of Shadows. It heard my thoughts and fantasies, and it wants to help me make them come true. All I need to do is perform the ritual.

Spell for Vengeance

First, obtain essential fluids of the body —
blood, spit, tears — from those you would harm,
and combine them in an elixir. Then in darkest night,
retire to a private room and disrobe entirely.

Face the south, and by the light of one black candle,
recite three times:

"Blood red, red blood, _sanguis hostilis_,

Better dead, choking blood, let the anger fill us.

Dead hand, dead heart, _mors hostili_:

We demand that you be cursed _et ad inferos_."

Consume the draught before the third recitation.

So mote it be.

SATURDAY, DECEMBER 17, 7:33 A.M.

God, I'm so scared. What have I done? I don't even know—my thoughts are so mixed up and confused. It's still dark out. Have I been asleep and dreaming this whole time? Or have I been up and wreaking havoc I only half remember?

The last thing I'm sure of is finding that spell for vengeance in my Book of Shadows. After that, things become hazy . . . I can see a black candle in my mind's eye, and a glass jar of murky liquid that I forced myself to drink. But could I really have gone out last night and collected blood, spit, and tears from all my enemies? And who were they? I have no memory of that.

After that, the visions in my mind are even worse. I can see . . . terrible things. Those awful creatures from my drawings—some with sharp claws, some with squelching fins and flippers, others with terrible beating wings. I watched them go out into the night and drag people from their beds. People I know! People like Madison and Betty and all their friends, but not only them . . . I saw Lara and Caleb and Lucas, too. I know I was angry with them last night, but would I have really named them among my enemies?

I don't know exactly where I was or how I was seeing these things, but somehow I was forced to watch the creatures perform horrible acts of torture on my friends. I watched them scream as their hair was set on fire, their teeth ripped out, and the flesh was torn from their bones.

And worst of all was that as I watched, I didn't feel horror or fear or sympathy for their sufferings. It felt wonderful. My whole body was so filled with spite and hate, there was no room for any emotion but delight and satisfaction as the creatures did my awful bidding.

And when they had their fill of torture, they dragged the bodies off into the shadows. But even now, I can still hear their screams echoing in my ears, along with the growling, crunching, and smacking of the creatures feasting on their prizes.

I know this has to be a terrible dream, right? But it feels so real, and I don't even remember going to sleep. I can see the sun is rising now, and it's terrifying to think that I have no idea what kind of world the daylight will bring.

SATURDAY, DECEMBER 17, 8:15 A.M.

Oh thank God, thank God. It wasn't real.

I was checking my phone for the time and realized the battery died last night. I plugged it in and found a whole bunch of messages from Lara and the others worrying about me—the most recent one from this morning.

So my friends didn't forget me after all. And the visions I described in my last entry, they must have all been a terrible nightmare.

I still feel shaken by the things I saw, though. And appalled that I ever thought for a second about performing that horrible spell the Book of Shadows suggested. Last night I was so ready to do it! Would it really have had the effects it had in my dream? How close did I come to cursing my best friends to torture and worse?

That book can't be trusted. I have to put a stop to it.

SATURDAY, DECEMBER 17, 8:53 A.M.

I'm not exactly sure what just happened. I woke up on the floor of my room with my head pounding.

I know after my last entry, I was working myself into a state, and thinking it would be for the best if I destroyed the book. But after that, things get sort of blurry. I remember noticing the knife I used before to cut out the page. It was still on my desk. And I had this idea that I could use that to . . . to *kill* the book. Except, the book's not alive. It's only an object, even if it's a powerful magical object.

I don't know. I have this image of myself stabbing into the book with the knife, over and over, as if I was trying to murder it. And I even can picture blood spurting out of it as if it was someone's chest, gushing all over my face and clothes.

But the next thing I remember is a heavy blow to my skull,

as if I'd run head first into a brick wall. And then I woke up on the floor.

There's no blood anywhere, and the book is fine—same as always. But I don't like what's going on with my mental state lately.

SATURDAY, DECEMBER 17, 3:25 P.M.

I went over to Lucas's today, but I'm back early. All I really wanted was to shake off the dregs of that terrible dream and feel normal again. But it made me feel worse.

I was too embarrassed by what happened at the dance to tell them about it, so I told them I wasn't feeling well that night and went home early. And I didn't tell them about the new spell in the Book of Shadows, or any of that.

I hoped that by keeping quiet about what happened, I could forget about it and move on. But of course they all wanted to talk about the dance and how much fun they had all night. And it wound up making me feel more left out then ever.

I know they're my friends, but there's this distance between us. I don't think they'll ever understand how different things are for me. Caleb has been one of the popular kids his whole life, and no matter how much he rebels, he still retains most of that. And Lucas has also always been well-liked and accepted, even when he came out of the closet. In fact, that only seems to have made him *more* admired by everyone at school. And even Lara—she basically chose her social position by making a statement about her beliefs that she knew would be controversial. She made the decision to take a stand against the mega-church kids, so whatever they throw at her, she can at least hold her head up and take pride in her commitment to her beliefs.

It's not like that for me. I've always been the outcast, and I always will be. Whatever rules people are willing to bend for the others are still firmly in place for people like me.

I wish there were a way I could have what they have—that easy self-confidence that comes from being generally respected, if not liked. Even if only for a day.

SATURDAY, DECEMBER 17, 9:24 P.M.

There's a new spell in the Book of Shadows.

I know I said I wasn't going to go near the book anymore, but tonight something drew me to it again. I can't explain it, but I had to look. And there it was: Spell for Glory and Renown. Which is pretty much what I was wishing for earlier. Sort of a fancy way of saying "popularity."

It's not a bad spell, either. I mean, the other one—the one for vengeance . . . that was clearly dark magic. I knew it as soon as I read it. Gathering bodily fluids from my enemies to bring harm to them? That's definitely in the realm of evil. But this one isn't so bad—more like the other spells we've done.

It made me wonder . . . after my nightmare, I became worried that the Book of Shadows was driving me to into darker and darker magic, to the point that it was beyond my control. But I don't think that's it. It's easy to blame the Book of Shadows for thoughts and impulses I'd rather not admit to, but ultimately, wasn't it trying to give me what I asked for? The whole vengeance thing was really my idea, because I was so angry when I got home from the dance. The Book of Shadows is nothing more than a tool, giving voice to my own thoughts.

And now that my thoughts are calmer, it's giving me a more reasonable spell to work with.

I know Lara keeps warning me against the Book of Shadows, and has become convinced it's only capable of black magic. But honestly, what does she know?

Let's look at the facts and try to be rational about this. Has the book ever done me or anyone else any harm? Other than a scary nightmare (which didn't really hurt anyone, and might have come from my own brain), so far all it's really done is boost my grades, get Caleb into college and liberate him from his asshole dad, give Lucas a boyfriend, and convince all the zealots in school to trade their bigotry for social justice. Even Tyler just got a boost to his popularity. That all seems really, unambiguously positive, so what exactly is Lara always so worried about?

It scared me to realize that what I thought were my own drawings were really coming from the book. But so what if they are? If the book wants to give me a special talent, don't I deserve that? Why shouldn't I trust the book's magic? As long as I only use it with good intentions, it will only produce positive effects. Whatever evil has been associated with the Book of Shadows didn't come from the book itself—it came from the greed, or pride, or vanity of the users.

As for this popularity spell, it doesn't seem very dark. I think it might really improve my life. I mean, is it so healthy for all my social connections to be in this one little circle? For me to be so dependent on them? We've been close friends for a while now, but they all have people outside the circle they can turn to if they need a break. Whereas for me—without the three of them, I'm all alone.

Besides, I'm tired of being treated like dirt every day in my own school. I tell myself I don't care what those people think, but it wears you down over time. Why should I have to live like that?

I know Lara wouldn't approve, but this is nothing like the scary magic of the vengeance spell. This is harmless. Anyway, it's not her book, it's mine, and I don't need her or the others for this spell.

Spell for Glory and Renown

Ink in blood the names of all whose admiration you seek.

Set the page aflame, and consume the ashes with water.

Focus your energy in a dark mirror and
repeat three times:

> "In the name of Astroth, may this draught
> bring me glory and renown."

So mote it be.

SUNDAY, DECEMBER 18, 11:12 P.M.

I did it—I did the popularity spell. Writing in blood is a lot harder than it looks in the movies. It doesn't exactly make great ink. I had to cut my leg with a razor blade to get enough, and then dilute it with some water to get it thin enough to work with. And dipping a pin into it wasn't the greatest writing implement, but I wrote enough names to be useful, I think. As long as I mark the major players, I'm sure everyone else will fall into line.

That is, assuming it works at all.

MONDAY, DECEMBER 19, 3:30 P.M.

Oh my God, it's working! It's really working! Even after so many proofs of its power, there was still a part of me that didn't believe the book would work for me. I can't believe I ever doubted it.

At first when I came into school, everything was the same as ever. Except I was avoiding Lara and the others. I don't know why, they haven't really done anything. I feel like maybe I've become too dependent on them for my social life. And maybe I was feeling a little guilty about doing a spell without them . . . but why should I? It's my book, and it's not like we ever had any kind of official agreement that we would all work together. Why shouldn't I do something on my own?

Avoiding my only friends in the world, made me feel more

isolated and alone than ever . . . kind of the exact opposite of the effect I was going for. I was sitting in class feeling sorry for myself, and as usual whenever I am stressed or sad, I found myself reaching for the Book of Shadows to start a new drawing. Which I do all the time and it's never been a thing, but for some reason this time someone noticed. Veronica Thompson— one of the most popular girls who would normally never even talk to me, unless it was to tell me that she was praying to save my soul from whatever sin I was supposedly committing that week.

Veronica came up to me and was clearly trying to get a closer look at the Book of Shadows. I hurriedly slammed it shut and tried to slip away before she could say anything, but she stopped me and asked if she could see what I was doing. And I froze like a cornered animal—exactly the kind of behavior that makes people avoid me. But I didn't know what else to do. I smelled a trap, of course—how could I not, given my experiences with Veronica and her kind? I didn't want to show her the drawing, but I didn't know how to get out of the situation without causing a scene, so I kind of . . . stood there. A deer in the headlights.

Somehow, out of all the unlikely possibilities in the world, Veronica must have taken pity on me. Because instead of spouting off her usual God-talk, she started telling me how she had been watching me work on the drawing all through class, and she found it really . . . *entrancing* . . . I think is the word she used. Said she'd never seen anything like it and wanted to see it up close.

Still, I couldn't quite believe what I was hearing. I was so prepared for her to do something sneaky or underhanded, like wait for me to show her the picture, then grab it and bring it to her pastor or some other church authority. All in the name of Jesus, of course. But when I continued to hesitate, she went on and asked if I'd ever had anything in the school lit mag. That at least broke me out of my paralysis, enough so I was able to say no. I mean, I've never even submitted anything. I never thought of myself as an artist until recently, and besides, that's another school group that is more or less run by the mega-church. They only support their own, so what would be the point for someone like me? I didn't say any of that, though—all I could manage was a simple "no." Veronica said she was coeditor this year, and she was looking for new work to include in their next issue. She said she wanted to see my drawings to see if they might use them!

That wore me down, so finally I consented to open the book for her to the page I'd been working on—a floating snake, with a gaping mouth full of sharp teeth. I was still suspicious, but also starting to feel a little excited and optimistic. And . . . well, unless she's playing a long game, it wasn't a trick! She loved the picture and she wants to include it in the next issue.

After that, we went back and forth a little bit about how I'd have to get her an electronic copy, and the right size and resolution and everything . . . administrative crap, but boy! It seemed like she was really serious! I was so stunned by the whole exchange that it didn't even occur to me to connect it with last night's ritual until later.

I can't believe this is any kind of coincidence. It can't be. And that means . . . well, if Veronica Thompson it talking to me now and acknowledging my existence, that's only the beginning. I didn't cast a spell to be in the school lit journal. I cast a spell to be popular. This is only the first stage. I'm so ridiculously excited to see where this might go! And I'm not going to lie, I'm a little terrified too.

THURSDAY, DECEMBER 22, 4:14 P.M.

Lara is pissed off with me now, because she figured out I'm using the Book of Shadows again. I suppose it was inevitably going to happen sooner or later.

I've been kind of ignoring her all week. Though if she texts me I do send a reply, and I still sit next to her in the classes we share. But I haven't been seeking her out like I usually do, and I found excuses all week not to join the others at Lucas's place. I haven't been eating lunch with them, either. Because Veronica invited me to eat lunch at her table, and well . . . that's what I wanted, isn't it? It feels good. It's nice to have other friends. I still like Lara and all them, but I hated feeling as if I needed them more than they needed me. I hated that sense of desperation I felt around them—the ugly awareness that they could all find other, better things to do, and I'd be left alone. Now I have options too. And what's wrong with that? It's definitely not like my old gang can't cope without me.

As for my new friends . . . I don't know. I don't always have that much in common with them, and sometimes their conversations make me feel like an alien visitor to their planet. Like when they talk about their daddies taking them to purity balls or whatever. Ick! I had no idea what to say to that conversation, except to thank God that my father doesn't view me as some piece of property to be kept pure from outside corruption. But on the other hand, they are also really welcoming and friendly and unnervingly upbeat about everything. It's difficult to fathom such cheeriness after spending so much time with brains (including my own) that tend to be cynical and skeptical about everything, and are always looking out for how we're going to get kicked in the ass. It's nice to be around more positive people for a change.

Part of me wonders if their lives seem better than mine *because* they are so positive about things. That maybe if you focus on the good, good things happen. Another, more cynical part of me wonders if it's easy to be positive when everything goes your way, for no good reason other than your family has money and you belong to the right church. At this point, I really don't know which side of me to trust. But I figure it can't hurt to get to know these folks better.

The point is, I've been avoiding Lara and the boys, and they finally noticed. Lara came up to me after school today as I was getting stuff out of my locker, and I was all ready to give her another excuse why I wasn't going to hang out this afternoon. But she spoke first and instead asked what was going on with me, pointing out that I'd been putting on a disappearing act lately. She asked if I was mad at her, and what she could do to make things better again. And dammit if she didn't seem really genuinely upset. I did feel pretty bad at that point, because I do miss her, and she didn't really do anything wrong. I know I was a little oversensitive about the popularity thing, and I can see now that she wasn't trying to tease me, she was looking out for me. If in a wrongheaded way. But I didn't really want to hurt her.

I was all set to patch things up with her, thinking that maybe I *would* go over to Lucas's today. Only then, Olivia Lang came up to us and started talking to me about the drawings I submitted to the art journal. Apparently she really liked them! She kept asking me questions about them, like where I got my ideas, and if I had taken classes for it. It was all a bit awkward because I could feel Lara bristling a bit over the whole conversation. She still thinks the drawings are evil, along with everything to do with the Book of Shadows. But I don't buy it. Even if they do come from the book, the drawings make me feel good, and other people enjoy them too.

But I knew Lara wouldn't approve, so I was trying to be nice to Olivia but also wrap the conversation up as quickly as possible to avoid tensions, when suddenly Olivia switches gears and says, "Hey, I don't know if you heard, but I'm having a party at my place New Year's Eve. You guys should come."

I didn't even know what to respond to that. I think I managed to stutter out some form of "Thanks," but I'm not even sure. I can't remember the last time I was invited to an actual party . . . maybe elementary school? It kind of goes with the territory of being an outsider. And this isn't any old party! This is most definitely a "cool kid" party—Olivia is really well connected and has a huge, fancy house. People are always talking about her parties at school on Mondays.

At that, Olivia smiled and left. Lara stood there as dumbfounded by the situation as I was before finally turning to me and saying, "Did Olivia Lang actually invite us to a *party*?" I shrugged like it was no big deal—as if getting invited to a Queen Bee party was an ordinary part of my existence. But I could see the wheels turning in Lara's mind, until finally she drew the obvious conclusion and asked if I'd used the Book of Shadows to perform another spell.

That pissed me off. Is it really so impossible that someone at this school besides Lara might want to spend time with me? That anyone might like me for me, and not because of some spell? I got defensive at that point and accused Lara of taking me for granted and not being able to accept that other people might actually like me. Which was dumb, I can admit now. Because Lara was completely right. Who am I kidding? I know I did the spell, and I know very well that's why people have been friendly to me this week. That's why Veronica asked to put my drawings in the art journal, and why people want to have lunch with me, and why Olivia invited me to her party. It has nothing to do with me. It's all thanks to that spell, like Lara said.

Still, though. It hurt when she pointed it out. I guess I wanted to live in my pretend world a little longer, and imagine that the Queen Bees liked and accepted me for me. But it's all an illusion, isn't it?

THURSDAY, DECEMBER 22, 9:17 P.M.

I had a long talk with Lara on the phone tonight and we worked
out some of our issues. She called first to apologize for suggest-
ing I couldn't have friends without the Book of Shadows. She
said that was unfair of her, and it was clear she felt bad about it.
That broke me down, and I had to admit that she was right. That
I did do that spell, and it *is* why people are being nice to me now.
I may have cried a little, because I am that pathetic.

Lara was quiet for a minute, but then she explained that her
suspicions that afternoon had nothing to do with me not deserv-
ing friends. Instead it had everything to do with what she knows
about Olivia and her group, how shitty and superficial they are,
and how incapable of appreciating actual decent human beings.
That did make me feel like less of a loser for needing magical

assistance to make friends. Maybe I could do it on my own if the Queen Bees weren't such wretched snobs. Lara, at least, is proof of that—I never had to trick her into being best friends with me. She's always liked me the way I am.

We made up and I apologized to Lara for doing the spell without her. I was ready to put the whole mess behind us. But then Lara asks, "So what about this party?" As if she thought I would actually go! I don't know. I was excited about it when Olivia asked, but once I accepted that those people don't really want me and are only under the influence of magic, that took some of the appeal away. It hadn't really occurred to me to go after that. But Lara said we should do it.

I was surprised—Lara has always been so opposed to the Queen Bees and everyone in that popular crowd. I didn't think she wanted anything to do with those people. But apparently she is at least curious. She hasn't been part of that "in group" since she was like eleven. So she doesn't know much more than I do about what that world is like. Except what Caleb has told her, of course. According to him, it's the most pathetic thing in the world to see a bunch of teenagers at a "party" with no alcohol, no drugs, no making out, and a ton of adult supervision. That made me wonder what exactly it is they do at these parties. Is it all pin-the-tail-on-the-donkey, like at a little kid party? Or prayer circles? It's hard to believe these are supposedly the "coolest" people in school, if their parties consist of standing around singing hymns for fun. I was starting to feel embarrassed that I ever wanted anything to do with the Queen Bees, but Lara convinced me we should go for the experience. Who knows when this spell will wear off? We may never get a chance like this again, and it might be educational to see how the other half lives. At the least, Lara assures me we can hang out in the corner and make snarky comments about all these church-obsessed weirdos.

So we're going? It should be . . . interesting, if nothing else.

SATURDAY, DECEMBER 31, 8:34 P.M.

Eep. I can't believe we're actually going to this party! I think I'm about ready, but Lara's still putting some finishing touches on her outfit, so I'm updating while I wait for her. We brought all our clothes and makeup over to Lucas's so we could share and evaluate each other's looks. This was probably a bad idea, though, because Lucas and Caleb were there, of course, and Caleb's been teasing us all night about going. He started regaling us with stories about how impossibly boring and lame these parties are, which is why he gave up on that popular crowd in the first place.

Oh well, I'm sure we'll manage to have fun anyway.

SATURDAY, DECEMBER 31, 9:03 P.M.

I just went to get a drink and Lucas cornered me in the kitchen. I'd noticed he'd been quiet all evening. I guess he was waiting for an opportunity to get me alone.

He doesn't think I should go to this party. I'm surprised at him—I thought he'd made his peace with all our spell work and concluded that it was all for a greater good. But something happened to him at the Winter Formal, he said. Nothing specific— more like a feeling that everything with Tyler and the dance and the activism was spinning out of control. He tried to convince me that the power we've been using is dark and dangerous.

I didn't see what any of this had to do with the party. Why should Lucas's guilt over his love spell keep us from having a little fun?

Lucas insisted that my popularity spell wasn't so different

from the one he performed on Tyler. He said there's no excuse for controlling and manipulating people to do something they normally wouldn't, whether it's to have sex or fall in love or be your friend. Doing it magically is no different from doing it with alcohol or drugs.

He said he thought I was better than that. That after he told me how torn up he was over the love spell, I'd think twice before doing something similar. Now that he's said that, I do feel bad that it didn't even occur to me. I didn't think wishing for more friends was anything like forcing a person to fall in love with you, but I see his point.

Still, what's done is done. Lucas has had plenty of time to enjoy the results of his spell—why shouldn't I enjoy mine for a while?

Forget him. I'm not going to let him ruin our evening.

SUNDAY, JANUARY 1, 1:27 A.M.

Jesus Christ, what a night. I hate to say it, but maybe I should have listened to Lucas's warning. Even though we never even touched the Book of Shadows, it's becoming more and more clear the effect it's having. And not only on us—this whole thing is getting bigger than I ever imagined.

Tonight was . . . It was so not what we were expecting. Given our past experiences, I think Lara and I were both figuring we'd show up to the party and be turned away, or have people freeze us out the whole time we were there. Or hell, maybe we'd even find ourselves walking into a prayer meeting where everyone tried to force some kind of conversion out of us. That'd be the worst, but hardly a surprise, in light of our history with this crowd. But it wasn't like that at all.

First of all, everyone was *really* excited to see us. Olivia seemed more afraid that we wouldn't show up than we were that they'd kick us out! And she was thrilled when we arrived. She started off apologizing that her kid sister, Emma, would be hanging around (Apologizing to us! Like, why would we care?) because Olivia was supposed to be babysitting her while her parents were gone. But she kept promising that Emma would stay out of the way and wouldn't get in the way of us "having a good time."

That was our first hint that this wasn't going to be as G-rated as their usual Christian youth-group style gatherings— the ones Caleb had described to us. Then Olivia showed us into the kitchen, where somehow she had managed to amass a whole party's worth of liquor. And you could tell she was really proud of the impromptu bar she'd stocked, and was hoping we'd be impressed. In the meantime Lara and I were both like . . . What did we walk in to? What kind of strange alternate universe is this?

The nearest I can tell, it's all connected to Lucas and Tyler getting together. It seems that ever since then, a lot of these hardcore mega-church kids have been questioning their assumptions and all the church teachings they've taken for granted all these years. And they've started experimenting. Which is . . . not what I expected! In a way, I feel a little bad about it, like our spell work has corrupted all their sweet, innocent souls. Only I know too well how *not* innocent they all were—innocent of alcohol, maybe, but not innocent of judging, bullying, gossiping, and preying on the weak and the different. If having a drink or two helps them shake off the rest of that garbage, I'd say it's a step in the right direction. Besides, drinking at parties isn't exactly outrageous behavior for normal teenagers.

The party was certainly awkward. Plenty of stilted conversation and uncoordinated dancing. But Lara and I were at least having a good time. It helped that everyone seemed so eager to seek us out and talk to us.

Then we figured out what they wanted to talk about. Olivia and Veronica and a couple of others cornered us on the deck at one point and were, like, "Um so, you guys are witches, right?" I know I was thinking, okay, yeah, that's it, they're going to throw us out now. They're going to turn on us or feed us some lecture about how we're going to hell. But no. These exact same people who made Lara's life so difficult for publicly admitting to being a follower of Wicca—these people now suddenly want to know everything about it. It's counterintuitive, but in a strange way it makes sense in the light of everything else we saw at the party. As far as they're concerned, supporting gay rights, drinking alcohol, and witchcraft . . . those are all things forbidden by their church. So if they're going to experiment with some of them, why not go all the way? And hell, I can't blame them for being curious. Especially after the sheltered lives they've all led.

At first they were only talking and asking questions about the craft—mostly polite ones, for a change. Like how Lara became a witch and what kind of books she has read and things like that. Then, someone asked for us to perform a spell. I suppose it was inevitable, especially as these lightweights started getting drunker. . . . Actually, what they said was a "magic trick," which really pissed Lara off. She was offended that they were treating us like circus animals, here to do party tricks for them. But I don't know, I didn't see it that way exactly. Maybe they were a bit clumsy in how they expressed themselves, but I think they

190

were sincere in their interest in Wicca. They just . . . didn't know enough to ask the right questions. But how can you blame them, given the way they've all been indoctrinated by that church?

So I talked with Lara a bit about what an opportunity this was. And she reminded me about how awful all these people had been to her when she first came out as Wicca, and I told her that of course she doesn't owe them anything after what they did. But obviously they did all that out of ignorance and fear and the brainwashing of their church. And if they were coming to her now, ready to learn and open their minds, wouldn't it be a shame to waste that? I mean, this could be a huge turning point for the school. Not only for Lara, but for the religious freedom of all the students who come after us.

That argument must have resonated with her, because she started to break down and agree that we should at least talk to them and educate them about the realities of Wicca. She still didn't want to do a spell, though—she said she'd had enough of spell craft for a while, and that she felt we needed to develop better control and magical awareness before we took it any further.

"Come on," I said. "What if we did something really simple and innocent, that couldn't possibly do any harm? It's the best introduction we could give them—otherwise it's all dry and abstract and academic. I promise, we won't even use the Book of Shadows. We'll stick to your old spells, from the books you know and trust."

Lara was hesitant, but eventually agreed that we could do a simple protection spell. Protection spells by their very nature are defensive, and are about guarding and preserving the practitioner's spirit, rather than trying to affect anyone else's or alter the patterns of the universe. So she couldn't see the harm, especially without the Book of Shadows involved.

Lara settled on a spell she knew from memory, and at first the popular kids seemed to want us to perform it for them, as if we were stage magicians. Like Lara thought they would. But she explained to them that real magic doesn't work that way— it's not a show you put on for an audience. And if they were really interested, they would have to participate. Some of them looked a little nervous at this, but after some hesitation, we convinced everyone to join hands in the living room, and Olivia dug up a pair of scissors and some emergency candles which we stuck into beer bottles and lit. Lara guided us through the simple ritual. She started by clipping off a lock of her hair and wrapping it in a length of plain white ribbon, reciting at the same time, "Spirits of nature, bind us and protect us from all who wish us ill." Then she passed the packet to the person next to her, who cut off a lock of her own hair and wrapped it together with the ribbon. We continued around the circle like this until everyone had done it, then we all held hands around the candle and repeated the incantation a few times before sitting in silence to focus our energy.

And that's when things got weird.

Before Lara even had a chance to say "So mote it be," that same energy we felt during the other spells started to hit me, but . . . ten times more powerful. No, twenty! It was so intense. It felt like the whole room was vibrating. I've never felt anything like that and I have nothing to compare it to. It scared me a little, even though it was also thrilling. I hadn't expected anything like that. I figured since this was such a simple spell, and we were doing it with all these people we have no emotional connection with, the energy would be much weaker than when it was only the four of us. But I couldn't have been more wrong. It was like we were practicing magic into an organic amplifier. Or like the horrible noises that come from putting a microphone too near its speaker. It nearly knocked me off my feet.

When I opened my eyes to see if I was the only one being affected in this way, it was clear that everyone else was feeling it too. I could see panic in Lara's eyes, which scared me, but the others were acting like they'd never experienced something so incredible.

At first I could only see it in the expressions on their faces, and maybe some twitching and trembling. But pretty soon I could see people were being overcome by the intensity of the energy in the room. Some of them started whooping and crying out, others were shaking, and Olivia even fell to the floor and started rolling around. That was just the beginning. Other people were convulsing and making strange yelps and sounds, tearing at their hair and clothes. Lara kept trying to get everyone to calm down, but at least a couple of people wound up naked on all fours or writhing on the ground, clawing at themselves, their eyes rolling back into their heads.

It was like nothing I'd ever seen before. In a matter of minutes, everyone had gone completely crazy. Betty Fillmore, the one who is always obsessed with the idea that I'm a lesbian, she grabbed me at one point and stared into my eyes. Her pupils were so big that her eyes were completely black. And she kept babbling, like, "Thank you, thank you. I've never imagined anything so beautiful in all my life." She was going on about "the spirit," and how the spirits in the room now were so much more powerful than anything she'd ever felt in church. And then, if everything wasn't strange enough, she took my face in her hands and kissed me! It was terrifying.

I was still scrambling to get away from her when Lara grabbed my hand and said, "We have to get out of here." We were down the stairs and on our way out the door when I suddenly remembered I'd left my bag behind. Lara told me we could come back and get it tomorrow, but the Book of Shadows was in there. Lara didn't say anything when I told her, but I could see in her eyes that she agreed it was a bad idea to leave the Book of Shadows with everyone in this state. So as quietly as we could, we crept back up the stairs and slipped into the back room where jackets and purses were kept.

When I walked in the room, I gasped at what I saw. Olivia's little sister, Emma, had gone into my bag and pulled the Book of Shadows out, somehow. That's the part that really scared me . . . Lara and I had gone into this party with the best of intentions, and didn't even touch the Book of Shadows the whole time. But somehow it found a way into our world all the same.

Emma was sitting on the floor with it, staring dreamily off into space as her pen moved around on the paper. I had this sudden, sick feeling of recognition looking at her—that must be what I look like when I do my drawings. Not like I'm concentrating really hard on some creative work, but like some outside force has taken over my body. It was disturbing.

Even more disturbing was the drawing itself—a strange creature with a goat's head and wings. It looked eerily familiar—

more so than most of my creatures, but I didn't take the time
to place it. I grabbed the book away from Emma and moved to
get out of there. Emma immediately started to cry and scream
about us taking away her beautiful drawing, but I didn't stop to
comfort her. I clutched the Book of Shadows to my chest as Lara
practically shoved me out the door.

SUNDAY, JANUARY 1, 2:47 P.M.

I wish I knew what to think about the Book of Shadows and the effect it's having on all our lives. Sometimes it seems like it has brought us so many good things, but then something happens and I'm reminded of how dangerous it can be. I worry that it's having an effect on my mind, and I don't know if I can trust my own judgment anymore. But if not, what *can* I trust?

I don't know exactly what's going on, but the power we've been playing with . . . it's bigger than any of us realized before. It's not just affecting us or even the people we cast spells on now—innocent bystanders are getting sucked in too.

Lara and I tried to explain this to the boys. Lucas seemed relieved that we'd come to the same conclusion as him, but I don't think Caleb got it. When I picture what happened at that party, it makes me shudder to think what we unleashed on that crowd. But Caleb seemed to think it was one big joke. He couldn't stop laughing at our descriptions of his old friends from the mega-church crawling around naked and making animal noises. He only seemed sorry that he had missed it.

Even when Lara told him about Olivia's kid sister drawing in my book, he didn't seem to grasp the full implications. That's when Lara explained why the drawing looked so familiar to me . . . it's not some random monster like the others. That goat-headed man is known as Baphomet, and it's a traditional representation of the Devil. She even pulled up a bunch of pictures on the Internet to show us how similar it looked.

As far as Lara is concerned, this is conclusive proof that we're not dealing with ordinary witchcraft anymore. There's nothing white about the magic coming from that Book of Shadows—the force behind it is the Devil himself. She thinks we have no choice anymore but to get rid of the book.

That pissed Caleb off, though. He started ranting about how unfair it was, that all the rest of us had gotten to pick a spell and do it, and he was the only one who hadn't gone. Which seemed a little ridiculous—I mean, is fairness really that important when we're talking about protecting our souls from demonic forces?

But the more Lara tried to get him to see reason, the more Caleb fought back. He said Lara sounded like the brainwashed idiots at the mega-church who are always convinced that everything is a demonic influence. Here we have this amazing power in our hands, and so far we haven't even really used it. He called all our spells so far "dumb kid's stuff," and a waste of a valuable resource. He said we needed to think bigger, be more ambitious.

But when Lucas asked him what he had in mind, he was at a loss. Meanwhile Lara was getting more and more upset about the way he was talking, and said this proved how much he had fallen under the book's influence. At that, Caleb calmed down and seemed to accept her point. He asked her how she proposed to get rid of the book, and she suggested bringing it back to the coven. At least they're real witches, and they have a lot more experience in these things. But Caleb nixed that idea. He said they were too weak and susceptible to corruption to be trusted with this kind of power. Even talking about the book had obviously stirred up strife among them and awakened their darkest impulses. The book could be incredibly dangerous in their hands.

I do see his point—after I saw the way they acted around the book, I don't much trust that coven either. But who else is there? What else can we do with it?

None of us could come to any good conclusion. At last Lara said we should drop the subject for a while and sleep on it. I went to pack the book into my bag, but Lara stopped me with a hand on my wrist. She suggested it might be better to leave it there, in Lucas's basement. Neutral territory.

I didn't really like being separated from it, but at the same time, my urge to have it near me at all times scares me a bit. So I agreed—it might be good for me to spend some time away from it. Good for all of us.

MONDAY, JANUARY 2, 5:42 P.M.

There's a new spell in the book.

I went over to Lucas's after lunch, since there's no school today, and the others were already there, debating where it came from. My first thought was that Caleb snuck in during the night and added it, but he denied it. And at this point, we'd be naive not to consider the more likely answer: the book is supplying its own spells again.

Regardless of where the spell came from, Caleb is now convinced that it was "meant" for him. This is the book's answer to his frustration about not being able to think of a suitable spell. This one Caleb likes. It's a spell for contacting the dead.

Lara said this spell is exactly the kind of magic we've been trying to avoid. It's necromancy, as any witch knows is the darkest sort of sorcery. But Caleb dismissed that idea. He said what makes magic dark is using it for a harmful purpose. There's nothing harmful in communicating with the dead. The dead can't be hurt worse than they are, and a spell directed at them has no effect on the living. It's no different from messing around with a Ouija board. He said this is exactly the spell we need—the one that will train us how to use the book. It will elevate us to the ranks of the adept, so we can truly control this power and bend it to our own will.

Lara was trying to come up with a counterargument for that, but Lucas settled the fight in a different way. He had the book out and was reading through the spell, and he told Caleb, "I don't think you're going to be able to do this spell."

He passed it around and . . . yeah. This spell is nothing like the ones we've been doing. This ritual is supposed to take place in a thirty-foot underground chamber made from "unblemished obsidian." That's not exactly something we have lying around. In fact Lucas was saying he figured no one had ever done this spell at all—that it was some magician's idea of a joke. An underground chamber like it was describing can't really exist. It would be beyond any human to carve something like that.

So I guess the argument is moot. If Caleb really wants to do a spell, he's going to have to find something else.

Spell for Summoning the Spirits of the Dead

In an underground chamber three yards square
made from unblemished obsidian,
place five black candles on an altar.

Focus your energies and repeat this incantation:

"In the name of Belial, Murmur, and Sabnock,
bring us the wisdom and knowledge of those
who came before us."

Place across the altar an offering of
rotted meat and sour wine and set it aflame.

So mote it be.

TUESDAY, JANUARY 3, 2:03 A.M.

I woke up a minute ago from the strangest dream. I was walking down a staircase somewhere. Even though it was pitch dark, somehow I knew it was carved out of stone and deep under the earth. I kept going further and further down into the ground until I saw a glowing light up ahead. I continued toward the light, and the stairs grew shallower until I found myself in a huge room carved out of black rock. And in the middle there were all these people wearing dark robes and holding candles.

I woke up then, and I was shivering all over, as if I could still feel the chill and damp of that strange room.

I know it's like the chamber in Caleb's spell. I must have conjured up the image in my dream.

It makes sense, since I was thinking about it before I fell asleep. But the strangest part is, I have this unaccountable impression that I know where it is—like if I were in a car, I could find it somehow. But how can a space like that even exist?

TUESDAY, JANUARY 3, 2:45 A.M.

I tried to go back to sleep after that dream, but I couldn't. I kept seeing those hideous creatures in the shadows around my room, and when I closed my eyes against them, I heard the snapping of their beaks, the ruffle of their feathers, and the scratching of their claws as they skittered along my walls. It didn't scare me, exactly, but I couldn't ignore it. It felt like they *wanted* something from me.

At last I tried texting Caleb, on the off chance he was up. He tends to keep odd hours. He answered my text right away, and asked me to tell him about my dream, so I called him. He agreed that it sounded like the place described in the spell, and he didn't think it was a coincidence. In fact, he said we should go try to find it.

"What are you talking about?" I said. "It's a dream. It doesn't exist."

But Caleb wouldn't listen to reason. He kept talking to me, in the soft, insistent voice of his, about astral projection and clairvoyance and all kinds of other odd phenomena, until it all almost sounded like it made sense.

Still, I resisted him. I even teased him a bit about how originally he'd been the ultrarationalist of our group, and now he apparently has become true believer in all kinds of supernatural activity—even after years of claiming that his own father's belief system was nothing but fantasy and delusion.

Caleb was silent a moment, and then he told me that wasn't quite true—or at least, that it wasn't the whole story, though he usually let people believe that's what happened. I knew he'd given up on his father's church when he was pretty young, and he told me before it was because he gradually realized he didn't share their faith. But he told me tonight it wasn't gradual at all . . . something happened back when he was a child preacher that changed everything for him.

He was maybe nine or ten years old when his dad was called in by a farm family out in the middle of nowhere who believed their teenage daughter was under the influence of demons. They wanted Reverend Gardner to "lay hands on her" and cast the demons out. Caleb's dad figured it would be a good learning experience for a preacher-in-training, so he brought Caleb along.

Caleb said he didn't take it too seriously at the time. He'd seen plenty of people in church possessed with the spirit, and privately he thought they were all faking for attention. He thought this would be a similar situation. So when they got there, he watched his father work with the girl for a while, and when Reverend Gardner needed a break, Caleb offered to step in. He liked being the center of attention, with all the desperate family members looking to him to save their daughter's soul. It appealed to his sense of drama.

But once he started going through the ritual, something changed. He went to the young woman and started to speak his bits of scripture at her, and he was shouting and gesticulating for all the world, but it was all a bit of theater to him. It never occurred to him that walking into this situation, he might encounter any real demonic influence. Then he laid his hands on her and looked into her eyes and . . . he saw something. And whatever it was, it wasn't the light of God.

It scared him. And for the first time he realized that maybe this wasn't all a game—maybe there really were forces in the universe that he couldn't begin to understand. He suddenly realized how vulnerable he was, and he couldn't go on. After that he declared the whole thing a fraud and refused to go to church anymore, but the truth was, it was the first time he'd ever considered it might be real, and it terrified him. He decided he needed to be as far away from it as he could get.

Eventually, enough time passed that he wondered if it had even happened. When he and Lara started dating, he was curious about her forays into witchcraft—he wondered whether she had ever encountered a force like the one he remembered. But nothing in her Wiccan practice seemed to have anything like the power possessing the girl that night. Nothing, that is, until we started playing with the Book of Shadows.

Up until I showed up with that book, he'd convinced himself that the whole encounter was nothing more than a kid's overactive imagination. But from that first ritual we did, and the energy it unleashed, Caleb suddenly started wondering again if it had been real.

At first, he was terrified—that's why he tried to dissuade us from doing that first spell. But the deeper we dove into it, the more curious he became about the nature of the power we'd stumbled on. He told me he made a mistake walking away all those years ago, and now he wants to know everything he can about this power—a power greater than anything his father conjures up in church.

Shit. My phone buzzed and I nearly jumped three feet in the air. Guess this whole conversation has made me a little jittery.

TUESDAY, JANUARY 3, 3:12 A.M.

It's a text from Caleb. He's outside my house! I can't believe this . . . it's the middle of the night and we have school tomorrow. But somehow he's convinced that I'm going to lead him to some magical cavern where he'll be able to communicate with the dead. What are we even doing?

This is ridiculous. I'm going to go down there and talk him out of it.

TUESDAY, JANUARY 3, 7:34 A.M.

I've been up almost the whole night—ever since that dream I had. I'll have to leave for school soon, but somehow I don't feel at all tired. I keep turning over in my head what happened tonight—honestly I don't know if I'll ever sleep again.

Obviously I didn't talk Caleb out of anything. I tried to—I swear I did. I reminded him of everything Lucas and Lara have said about using magic to exploit and manipulate people against their will. But Caleb wasn't impressed. He said if there's one thing living in this town has taught him, it's that most people are sheep, desperately looking for someone to guide them. Left to their own devices, they'll follow someone like his dad. "Isn't it our duty to offer them a better option?" he asked.

I don't know. In the light of day, it doesn't sound like a great argument, but last night in Caleb's car it made sense. I knew he was turning his preacher charm on me, but for the first time, I didn't want to resist that look, that voice, like we were the only two people who mattered in the world. Something stirred in my blood, and I knew that wherever Caleb was going with this, I wanted to be there too.

With the Book of Shadows clutched closely to my chest, I didn't even have second thoughts when I noticed the awful smell coming from the backseat, though maybe I should have. Caleb explained that on an impulse, he'd gathered together the rest of the materials we'd need for the spell: a handful of black candles, some sour wine, and rotting meat that he'd picked out of the Dumpster behind the church's food kitchen. I still thought it was pretty optimistic that we'd find the place, but I guess he wanted to be prepared.

Once I agreed to go along with Caleb, he sat there behind the wheel, staring at me expectantly. Then I remembered that I was supposed to be guiding this little mission. I felt really foolish there for a minute, because here I had gotten him out in the middle of the night, and I had no idea what our next step was. But I couldn't back out at that point, so I picked a direction and told him to drive. And then, when we came to an intersection, I picked another direction. It felt really random at first and I thought any minute Caleb was going to call me out as a fraud. But he didn't, and as we drove on, it somehow became easier. I don't know how to describe it exactly, but I felt this strange . . . pressure inside of me every time we reached a turn, and somehow I *knew* the right way to go. And while at first I was half convinced that I was deluding myself, I gradually grew more and more confident that we were going the right way. Especially once we left the highway and started following these back roads toward an area where I knew there were cave entrances.

And that's exactly where my directions took us . . . not to the main entrance, where during the day there are signs and ticket takers for tourists visiting the caves. We wound up on this road in the middle of nowhere that was pretty gloomy and desolate. I told Caleb to stop the car, and he did, but I could tell that he was less sure of my instincts than he had been. But as for me, I was more certain than ever that we were on the right track. That inexplicable pulsing pressure in my chest was getting stronger and stronger, and it pushed me to trek through a field and up a bramble-covered rise, Caleb following behind me. And there it was—hardly more than a chink in some rocks, but wide enough that we could both slide through it. We had to shimmy through the tight passageway for a few feet before it opened up into a larger cavern.

We had stupidly forgotten to bring any flashlights, but Caleb lit one of the candles and illuminated the space we were in. It was small—much smaller than that promised by the spell, but we could hear running water and see a place where the ground sloped down. I headed there, only to find that the shallow depression gradually turned into what was clearly a staircase leading deep down under the earth. We followed the stairs until they leveled off into a tight, low corridor. It was only then that I really started to get nervous that we were on the wrong path, because everything seemed to be closing in and getting smaller, and there was no sign of the cavern we were looking for.

But just when I was going to suggest maybe turning back, there was a twist in the passage, and when we turned the corner we were suddenly in a much larger space—too large to be defined by our single candle, in fact. I felt along the walls for a bit, trying to get a sense of the size, and that's when I realized unlike the rest of the caves (or any cave I've ever heard of), the walls were perfectly smooth and straight, as if they had been painstakingly carved out of the living rock. The floor was too. And when I reached a corner, I could tell that it made a perfect ninety-degree angle. This had to be the place we were looking for.

Caleb was way ahead of me, of course. He'd already noticed that in the center of the room was a rectangular stone that rose about a foot and a half from the floor level. This, he decided, must be the altar, and he went about setting up his candles and other materials on it. Once the other candles were lit, I could see clearly that the room was unlike anything I'd seen before—it was exactly as the spell had dictated, three yards square in every direction, and cut clean from smooth, black, unblemished stone.

I couldn't believe that such a structure could exist here in this cavern without anyone knowing about it. Had it been here for centuries? Had it been used before by previous generations of witches? Or did it spontaneously appear tonight, in response to my dreamed request?

I kept staring around the chamber in awe, but Caleb didn't waste any time getting the ritual started. I could see he was intent on pushing this strange experience to its limits. Once the candles were set up, he directed me to stand across the altar from him and begin the incantation. After a few repetitions, he took one of the candles and touched it to the slimy meat he had brought until it started to burn and release a foul smoke into the air. It was gross and I wanted to cough, but I kept chanting.

After a while I closed my eyes against the prickling smoke, and when I opened them again, I could make out the shape of someone else in the cave with us. What looked like an old man in a long dark robe was standing outside the circle of light cast by our candles. Glancing over at Caleb, I could tell that he had seen him too, and after a couple more repetitions, we both stopped chanting.

For a while, we stood there in silence. I felt a sick, cold fear running through my whole body. In all the rituals we had done so far, we had never experienced anything like this. Nothing ever happened during the ritual itself other than some kind of sub-jective feeling—energy and vibrations and that type of thing. Even afterward, all the effects we saw were things well within the laws of physics—things that could have other explanations besides our magical practice. But this? A man showing up in this underground chamber, where before there had been no one? It was impossible—even more impossible than the existence of the chamber itself.

I couldn't help think back to Lara's warnings about necro-mancy and black magic. What had up to now been a fun, harm-less game suddenly seemed much more serious.

At last Caleb spoke—it was more than I could have done, though I noticed his voice was choked and trembling. He asked the figure to say his name, and where he came from. But the man didn't answer. Instead he paced solemnly into the circle of light cast by our candles, and extended an arm toward Caleb. Caleb stared at him for a moment or two, then as if in answer to some silent signal, he sank to his knees and bowed his head. The man rested a hand on Caleb's forehead and I saw his lips move as if reciting some prayer or incantation, though he made no noise.

Then he turned to me and for the first time, I had a clear

view of his face. It was wrinkled and spotted with age, but piercing blue eyes peered out at me from under his heavy hood, and they struck me with a sense of calm power. When he held out his arm toward me, I felt no fear, only excitement as I fell to my knees and let him press a hand to my skull.

After a few moments, I felt him take his hand away, and I lifted my head to look at him again. The man had stepped back into the shadows, but he was now not the only unfamiliar figure in the room. Advancing from the shadows were maybe a dozen others—some women, some men, some old, some young. Many wore robes like the old man, but the rest were dressed in other strange costumes—dark suits and dresses in styles from many different centuries. At first, they only milled around aimlessly, making occasional wordless signs at one another. From time to time I saw one of them glance in my direction or at Caleb, and each time the person would give a slight nod before moving on.

Then at last the crowd formed itself into a loose circle around the altar, dense and dark enough that I didn't have a very clear view of what was going on within. But as people moved around, I caught glimpses here and there of someone stepping into the candlelight to place a black carved goblet on the table, and another person stepped forward and placed a gleaming dagger alongside it. Finally the first man we saw—the one who had touched our heads—came forward with an odd shaped bundle in his arms, and this too he placed on the altar.

I watched curiously, trying to figure out what it was, and then a shriek split the air of the cavern and suddenly I knew. The bundle he had placed on the altar, which I now saw was squirming slightly in its wrappings—it was a human baby.

I held my breath in dread of what was going to happen next,

but I felt frozen in place, totally unable to stand and stop the scene in front of me. And as I watched the circle in horror, wondering if anyone else would step forward, I realized something had changed. The human faces of the assembled crowd seemed to shift and distort in the flickering candlelight, and I could swear that among them I saw eyes grow bulbous and dark, skin turn slimy with scales, and teeth lengthen into horrible shards.

Suddenly there was a flash of light as a clawed hand raised the dagger, and it plunged down with one swift blow, suddenly silencing the infant cries that had filled the room.

I think I must have fainted or blacked out at that point, because the next thing I remember, I woke up coughing from the rancid smoke that now filled the room, and Caleb was pulling me to my feet by the light of a single candle.

I looked around and saw that the room was now empty, and other than the remnants of meat and wine that we had brought, there was no sign of the crowd of people I'd been watching only moments before. I didn't pause to question it, I grabbed the Book of Shadows and followed Caleb out of the chamber, back up the rough stairs, and through the cavern to the open air.

The night was dark, but somehow we found our way back to the car, and Caleb started us home. So many times on that trip, I turned to him to ask what had happened, and if he had seen the same things I saw, and how much of it was real. But each time I looked over at him, I somehow couldn't find the words. So we made our drive in silence.

TUESDAY, JANUARY 3, 3:32 P.M.

School was surreal today. After everything that happened last night, I wasn't even thinking about the fallout from the New Year's Eve party. I think we were smart to get out when we did, because apparently the whole thing pretty much exploded after we left. I mean, even more than it already had.

A neighbor wound up calling the police with a noise complaint at some point, which led to the police contacting Olivia's parents, who came home to be confronted with this bizarre scene that must have looked like a Satanic orgy to them. Which I suppose isn't all that far off the mark.

All the mega-church kids are in big trouble now with their parents and with the church. Once I heard the gossip, I did my best to lie low, figuring everyone would be angry with me for getting them into this situation. But I was wrong. Everyone in school is vying for my attention today. People who were at the party want me to explain what happened, and why. People who weren't at the party want to know how they can join the fun—I've never received so many invitations in all my life. They all want me to share my secrets and set up another so they can experience it too. But I don't even understand what happened that night! I don't know where that energy came from, and I have no idea how to reproduce it, even if I wanted to.

In the meanwhile, all I can think about is what happened in that cave last night. At lunch, I finally caught up with Caleb to talk about it. But I don't think he has a much clearer idea of it than I do. I *think* we saw some of the same things, but neither of us wanted to go into too much detail. In any case, Caleb seemed to think that whatever happened was somewhere between a séance and a hallucination. Maybe something like peering into the past.

I don't know if that's the best explanation. I can only hope that what happened to that baby was a piece of pure imagination.

One thing he was sure of, though—that the people who gathered in that chamber last night were the previous masters of the Book of Shadows, answering the call of our ritual. And that by their gestures, they were welcoming us into their ranks.

As for what happened at the end, when their faces and bodies turned monstrous . . . I wanted to ask him about that too, but I didn't. I was afraid to have that part confirmed by him.

I know this is the last thing I should be doing right now, but I found myself pulling out the Book of Shadows later in the day at school and starting a new drawing—an ancient, wizardy-looking beast in a cowled robe, with wrinkled, grasping hands. I wasn't even in a trance this time—I did it consciously, deliberately.

I know it's a bad idea, but after last night I needed something to calm my nerves, and lately this is the only thing that works.

THURSDAY, JANUARY 5, 3:12 P.M.

I'm feeling a little better about our ritual the other night. Honestly it scared the hell out of me at the time, but Caleb has calmed me down about it. He says I've become overly fixated on Lara's distinctions between "white magic" and "black magic," when really, it's not like there's any clear-cut line.

We talked about the mega-church, and how they present themselves as all righteous and pure and on the side of good, but in the meantime I've watched its members do terrible, mean-spirited, and hypocritical things in the church's name. Just because something calls itself "white" or "good" is no reason to trust it.

The same goes for things that get called "black" or "dark." It's a matter of perspective, really. The Book of Shadows has given us power, and most people are afraid of power, so they automatically call it dark. But power in the right hands can accomplish a world of good.

He says I should worry less about the source of the power, and more about what I'm doing with it. As long as we haven't done any real harm, we have nothing to feel bad about.

MONDAY, JANUARY 9, 3:22 P.M.

Oh God. Drama, drama.

Not that I wasn't expecting it, but, I had kind of hoped that Caleb could keep the ritual we did as our little secret, at least for a while. We never explicitly said we would, but he knew very well that Lara and Lucas didn't want us messing with the Book of Shadows anymore, so I assumed he would not mention it to them or anyone else. But I should have realized that's not Caleb's way. As soon as I got to school this morning, I knew something had changed.

As long as I've known him, Caleb has always gone out of his way to avoid the Queen Bees and all the other brain-washed zombies from the mega-church. But today I saw him out in the school parking lot with a small crowd around him. He wasn't telling them about our ritual, exactly, but he was talking about methods and techniques of performing magic, and of course people were hanging on his every word. No surprise there, since not only was he discussing a topic a lot of people are interested in these days, he was using his preacher voice. It was really something—I'd never seen him use it in front of a whole group before. It's remarkable how that same intensity and intimacy he brings to private conversations somehow swells to meet every individual in a group. Watching him, I understood what his father had seen in him—he could certainly make an awe-inspiring preacher.

I stood watching him awhile, as transfixed as the others, until I noticed Lara approaching from the other direction. She stopped and listened when she saw what Caleb was doing, and I could see the realization dawn on her face as she figured out what we had done. She was livid. She wouldn't talk to me all morning, and when I tried to approach her at lunch, she gave me this huge lecture about messing around with forces I didn't understand, and taking huge risks, and exposing ourselves to all kinds of negative influences.

I let her go on for a while because a part of me agrees with her—the part that was pretty disturbed by what happened during our last ritual. But eventually it started to get to me. Who is she to lecture me? What gives her the right? Because she was into Wicca before me? Does any of that even matter anymore? Caleb is right—it really doesn't matter how much time she has spent with her books, because when it comes down to it, it's the practice of magic that's the measure of a witch, not the theory. Anyone can spout theory, but if they can't produce magical effects, what good are they? Caleb and I have now done some of the most advanced and difficult magic out there. And Lara hasn't—I mean, honestly, what has Lara even contributed to our little coven other than that silly good luck spell in the beginning? We came up with all the other spells without her help.

I think Caleb is right—Lara is jealous that we've become better witches than she ever was on her own. She wants to put the genie in the bottle so she can go back to being the special, unique one. But we're the ones with real power now, so why should we answer to her?

WEDNESDAY, JANUARY 11, 4:02 P.M.

When it rains it pours. . . . Our little drama seems to be spreading to the rest of the school. Everyone's still talking about the aftermath of the New Year's Eve party. I've been avoiding it as much as possible because I'm sick of talking to people about it when I don't even fully understand what happened myself. But I found out today that Caleb's dad pulled all kinds of strings to keep the party off the TV news, because it would be such a huge embarrassment to the mega-church. Think about it—a story about how the best and brightest teens from the church's youth group had been discovered in the middle of some black magic ritual. (Not that it was actually black magic, but I can't imagine the news or the general public would make any fine distinctions.) A story like that would go viral in minutes, and would be national news by tomorrow. Caleb's dad and the mega-church would be in disgrace.

Put that way, I can understand why Caleb was so excited about it. He lives for anything that reveals his father's weaknesses.

Since then, there's been this huge effort on the part of the adults to hush everything up—in fact, they seem more concerned about that than actually punishing anyone, which is interesting. But if you ask me, it's too little too late: that church may well have a revolution brewing among its younger members. Now that they've seen a little bit of the other options out there, they're not exactly rushing to "return to the fold." There have been all kinds of behavior problems this week, with people acting out who never would have dared before. They've started dressing differently—I've seen more people wearing black nail polish and heavy metal T-shirts in the past week than in the last three years of school. A couple of kids even approached me about using some of my drawings to base tattoos on. Can you imagine? Even *my* parents would go off the deep end if I got a tattoo like that. I don't even know how some of those hyper-conservative church people would react. But I have to admit, it was cool and kind of flattering to be asked.

Still, I can't help judging them a bit for thinking they can suddenly turn around and buy their way into the craft via hair dye and mall fashion. After all the time and effort we put into our magical training, and these newbs are trying to pass themselves off as adepts? But at least it's fun to sit back and watch the havoc they're unleashing.

On a less happy note, Lucas and Lara are still not talking to me. I miss them, but I don't believe I have anything to apologize for—Lara especially was being controlling and had no right to dictate to me how I use my own Book of Shadows. Anyway, I have loads of new friends now—friends who think I'm super-cool and hang on my every word.

Which is a nice change of pace. Though even with my popularity spell, they don't swarm around me the way they do around Caleb. I never thought of him as someone who was at all interested in popularity, or what people think of him. After all, he had plenty of chances to be popular, and he walked away from all that to do his own thing. But he's really changed since we did that ritual together. Oh, he still doesn't give a crap about superficial popular kid stuff like going to parties or getting nominated to prom court, but I think he's getting a real kick out of letting people know he's a magical adept. It's something to see every lunch period, when a group gathers around him to ask questions about the practice and theory of witchcraft, and he alternates between sitting on one of the tables or pacing energetically back and forth in front of the mega-church kids hanging on his every word. It's almost like he's assembling his own congregation of wannabe witches to rival that of his father.

I can tell Lara thinks Caleb is becoming as bad as his father, but she's overreacting. Nothing *really* bad has ever happened from any of our spells—I mean, no one we enchanted has complained. So what is she so worried about? Sometimes I think all she really cares about is being the expert of our group. She's only pissed because she can't control us anymore.

TUESDAY, JANUARY 17, 3:45 P.M.

Oh shit. SHIT. I've really done it this time. I don't know what I'm going to do! I've lost the Book of Shadows.

It's all my fault. It's my most precious possession—the most precious thing I can even imagine owning in my whole life. How could I take it for granted? How could I let it go so easily? I've been such an idiot. I should have seen this coming.

It all started because I was drawing in class—the way I've done a million times, the way I do all the time now. But I used to be more careful about it, a little more subtle. I never really worried that much about being caught by a teacher—I think it was more the other kids hassling me that I was nervous about, so I tried to hide it from them. But ever since my drawings appeared in the school lit mag and everyone went wild about them, I haven't worried about that so much anymore. I'm kind of proud of them now, and if people want to look over my shoulder while I work or whatever, I let them.

Well, that's what happened today. I was in history class and had the book out and I was adding a new picture of a beast with a layered carapace and a devilish-looking hooked nose, and some of the people around me were peering around to look and asking questions about it—not really being that subtle. But I wasn't discouraging them either. I was enjoying it.

That's when I got caught. I didn't even realize Mr. Peters had noticed what I was doing until he was standing right next to me and snatching the book off my desk. He looked at the picture for a while, then flipped through and looked at the others, one by one. He said something like, "What is the meaning of this?" but I was so upset I couldn't even answer.

Still, I thought at most he might put it in his drawer and give it back to me after class. But it was so much worse than that.

He took the book and told me to stay after the class ended. Even at that point I still wasn't too worried. But once the bell rang he stepped outside to make a phone call, then escorted me down to the principal's office.

That's when things really went off the rails. Because what I didn't know was that both Mr. Peters and the principal are members of the mega-church. Obviously. I mean, why wouldn't I assume that? More than half the teachers at school are, which I knew in the abstract, but I'd never had much reason to think about which specific teachers were, since most of them are pretty careful to obey at least the letter of "separation of church and state" during school hours. But apparently today they decided to throw all that out the window for the sake of my immortal soul. Mr. Peters showed the principal my Book of Shadows, and of course between my drawings and the handful of spells we've written down, they both completely lost their shit. They started haranguing me about inviting the Devil himself into the classroom; I kid you not. It was *so* hard to keep from rolling my eyes, and I think I may have failed once or twice, which only made the situation worse.

Then the principal excused himself to make a phone call, and I assumed he was calling my parents. Which I wasn't all that concerned about, because they don't belong to the megachurch, and they'd never believe anything about Devil worship. But ten minutes later, who shows up? Not my parents. Caleb's dad! It was so bizarre, I didn't know what to say or think at first. I swear I had this disorienting moment where I wondered if they were confused about whose parents were whose, or if Caleb had somehow coincidentally gotten into trouble too. But pretty soon it became clear that Reverend Gardner wasn't there at all in his capacity as a parent—he had been asked there as a man of God.

After what happened at that party, I might have known all the crazy mega-church folks would be on super high alert. He was probably trying to figure out if I knew who it was who had been corrupting all the town's innocent youth. And in a way, I *am* the one who has corrupted everyone—none of this would have even started if not for me stealing that blank book from the used bookstore and bringing it to school. But I definitely didn't tell him that. And I didn't point fingers at anyone else, either—I tried to downplay everything I could, saying I'd found the spells on the Internet and it was all just for fun. A game. Which made them even angrier, because how could I treat this as a game and didn't I know how dangerous this was? Blah blah blah. It's actually funny how much they sounded like Lara, especially given that she's like their arch nemesis. But as long as I at least played innocent, there was only so much they could do.

So *finally* after about an hour of that, they did call my parents, which was a huge relief, because I thought I'd finally get out of this hell. But they knew better than to launch into their Devil warnings to someone like my mom. Once she walked in, they changed their tune completely and simply said I hadn't been paying attention in class, and had been distracting the other students.

So I had to sit through a lecture about that from all sides, plus they gave me a day's detention, then sent me back to class. But before I went, I politely asked when I could get my book back. And Reverend Gardner said, "I think it's best if we confiscate that item permanently. It's providing too much distraction from the studies of you and your fellow students."

I tried to tell them, no way—it's my property, they can't keep it. But my mom agreed with them—she said that I *had* been distracted lately and not focusing on my schoolwork, and that I shouldn't be doodling in this book during class, so I was better off without it. And that was that!

There was nothing I could do. They sent me back to class and Caleb's dad took off with my Book of Shadows. What am I going to do? I have to get it back!

WEDNESDAY, JANUARY 18, 12:15 P.M.

I tried to get in touch with Caleb, but he was not answering his phone. But I finally tracked him down today and told him what happened. I expected him to be pretty pissed that I allowed the Book of Shadows to fall out of my hands, but it turns out he had his own problems to deal with. Reverend Gardner has been searching for whoever has been "corrupting the town's youth" ever since that party Lara and I went to. And once he actually showed up at the school he learned that his own son has been boldly promoting witchcraft and ritual magic throughout the school.

Caleb and his dad have had issues for a long time, and Reverend Gardner was definitely aware that they had differences when it came to church matters. Up to now, though, he'd always looked the other way in public in order to keep Caleb from tarnishing his and the church's good name.

This latest outrage, however, turned out to be the final straw. Caleb and his dad got into a huge screaming fight in the parking lot, hurling passages of scripture at each other as if their souls depended on it. And when all was said and done, Reverend Gardner kicked Caleb out of the house!

He's not sure what he's going to do now, though Lucas has said he'll talk to his parents about letting Caleb stay. I tried to tell Caleb that it might be for the best—that it might end up being a more stable and sane environment for him than his parents' house ever was. To my surprise, Caleb actually seemed upset about the escalating tensions between him and his father. They've always had such an adversarial relationship, I figured Caleb would be happy never to see him again. But I suppose it's hard to give up on family altogether.

Anyway, Caleb didn't have much useful advice for getting the Book of Shadows back. I had hoped he'd be able to, I don't know, sneak into his dad's office and take it back, but obviously that's not going to be possible.

Besides, Caleb says his father takes anything to do with witchcraft, black magic, or the Devil extremely seriously. Which shouldn't surprise me, given his occupation, but Caleb says that means he's not about to leave an intensely magical object lying around on his desk. Caleb seemed certain that his father would immediately look into ways to destroy the book, if he hadn't done so already. He would know something—some prayer or holy ritual he could perform—that would knock the magic out of the Book of Shadows once and for all, and render it useless.

And if that didn't work, he'd burn it. Anything to make sure no one would ever use it again.

I can't help it—I felt an ache deep in my chest when he told me that. My book! It doesn't seem fair that some random person should be able to destroy something that has meant so much to me. To us. And all my drawings! When I thought of them curling with flame and turning to ash, I almost started crying. All those hours I spent on them . . . I've never created anything like that before. How can this man take all that away from me, just like that?

But at the same time, I have to admit there's a part of me that's a little bit relieved—the moment the book passed out of my hands, it was almost like a dark cloud lifted from over me. That last ritual I did with Caleb really was thrilling, but I can't help thinking of all Lara's warnings about how we were getting in over our head, and letting the Book of Shadows have too much control over us. And that scene at the party . . . I'm convinced there was something malevolent at play that night. I could feel it in my blood.

The powers in that book were greater than any of us fully understood, and definitely more than we could control. Maybe it's safer to have it in the hands of someone like Reverend Gardner. If he has the strength and the knowledge to destroy it, maybe in the end that's for the best. God knows I didn't.

THURSDAY, JANUARY 19, 5:45 P.M.

One good thing did come out of me losing the book at least—
Caleb and I have made up with Lara and Lucas. The Book of
Shadows was the main point of contention between us. Lara
wanted us to quit messing with it altogether, Caleb wasn't
willing to give up the power it promised, and I always found
myself torn between the two positions. In the end, I always
went back to the Book of Shadows. Which pissed Lara off,
understandably.

With the book out of the picture, that's not an issue anymore. Maybe it's just as well that we can't play with it anymore.
It was a thrill to perform all those spells, and see our intentions
made into reality through magic, but it was scary too. Now that
the book is out of my hands, I'm starting to see how much it
clouded my thoughts. As long as it was in my room, I could

never seem to resist its temptations. I miss it, but I also feel safer now that it's gone.

I haven't seen any of those fantasy beasts anymore, either, since Reverend Gardner took the book. I miss them a bit, but at least I'm sleeping better. I wonder . . . does the fact that they've receded mean Reverend Gardner has already neutralized the magic in the book? Or is the book focusing its influence on its newest owner?

I don't know, but now that it's out of my hands, I don't really care. The most important thing is I have my friends back, and everything can get back to normal now.

FRIDAY, JANUARY 27, 7:15 A.M.

.

There's something strange going on in this town, and I think it might have something to do with the Book of Shadows. Caleb was so certain that his father was going to destroy the Book of Shadows, and I thought that would be the end of it. But now I'm not so sure.

It was Lucas who noticed what was happening first. Ever since his parents realized that the church included them only to up their "diversity quotient," they pretty much lost interest and started only going for major holidays. He says his family always thought of the church as a useful social network, but they've never exactly been ardent believers.

But something changed this week. Not only did they get up and go to church this past Sunday, they tried to make Lucas go too. And when they returned, they started hounding him about how he was endangering his soul by straying from the church teachings. They've *never* said anything like that before. At first he thought they were kidding, but all week they've been sounding like a couple of True Believers.

If that was all there was, I don't know that I would make too much of it. For all the time I spend at their house, I've never gotten to know Lucas's parents that well. Maybe they had a change of heart, who knows? But there's more.

Like on Tuesday, the news reported that the mayor of the city joined the mega-church and participated in a big baptism ceremony. The next day, the whole city council had a mass baptism. In fact, all week, all the news online and on TV has been about these mass baptisms of practically anyone with any power in town. Then it came out yesterday that both the city newspaper and the local TV affiliate have been bought by the church—for a ridiculously low amount.

It's like the whole town is being taken over, and anyone who isn't a member of the church is starting to feel nervous. I've heard rumors about local business owners being told they'll need to convert or leave town.

Who does that sort of thing? Even compared to everything we've experienced, this feels surreal. This town has been under heavy influence from the church for as long as I can remember, but there have always been holdouts like my family. . . . Enough so that you didn't feel like the church had *complete* control. But now?

There's something really unnatural about how quickly all this is happening. I didn't even feel surprised when Caleb said it out loud: his father must be using the Book of Shadows to influence people. I don't know if he's doing it deliberately, or if the power is seeping out somehow, but it's the only possible explanation.

And if that's the case . . . I'm scared to think of where all this leads. Right now it's a bunch of people joining a respectable Christian church, and no one outside of town is likely to be too shocked by that. We do live in the Bible Belt, after all. But if the forces behind that book are what Lara's been saying . . . this could be the beginning of something much darker.

I feel like we need to do something to stop this before it takes that turn. But what?

FRIDAY, JANUARY 27, 4:13 P.M.

It looks like the rumors I heard are true—the ones about businesses being run out of town if they won't conform to the church and the new city leadership. There was a big list on the front page of the paper this morning of all the businesses that are considered "enemies of the church," and some veiled threats about rents and taxes and fines.

In fact Lara pointed out that one of the names on the list this morning was White Rabbit bookstore. She was particularly furious about that because it's always been her favorite store, and she says the owner, Derek, is a really good person. To which Caleb made a comment—something like, "What goes around comes around," and my heart sped up a little knowing what was going to come next. Of course Lara wanted to know what he meant, because after all this time, I still haven't told her where the book came from. And I guess, for all his promises, Caleb is no longer interested in keeping my secret.

From across the room, Caleb shot me a meaningful look. For a moment, I scrabbled around mentally for a way to keep Lara in the dark about what I'd done all those months ago. But I realized Caleb was right—the time for hiding such things is over. What seemed like a shameful crime a few months ago is hardly worth keeping secret in light of everything that has happened since.

I decided to come clean. I told Lara I got the book from White Rabbit. She looked at me sort of confused, and I cleared my throat and clarified: I *stole* it from White Rabbit.

I expected Lara to tell me that was a rotten thing to do, and that would be the end of it. But she didn't view it as such a small thing, apparently. She was quiet for a bit, then she became grave and serious. She pointed out that by stealing the book, I had imbued it with dark energy—like Rosemary and Bob did when they brought the book back from Europe. She said that was probably what gave some evil entity the toehold it needed to break into our world. I reminded her of the cleansing ceremony she performed back when I first brought it home—wasn't that supposed to take care of any dark energy? But Lara said it doesn't work that way. You can cleanse an object's history, but you can't cleanse your own bad deeds from it without making some kind of amends.

Well, how was I supposed to know any of that? But I suppose if I had admitted to her earlier how I'd come to possess the book, maybe we could have dealt with this issue before it became so big.

I felt terrible when I realized that. It was so cowardly and vain of me to keep this secret. I should have trusted Lara, and been honest with her, instead of hiding this out of embarrassment.

It would be easier, in a way, if Lara were mad at me, but that's not her way. I can still see her dark eyes, not angry, but worried and disappointed, because of me. At first, I was upset that she was treating me like a criminal about what seemed like no big deal. But she's right, isn't she? This whole mess was really caused by my one thoughtless, selfish decision that afternoon.

I don't know what to do. I want to make amends, but I don't know how. And I couldn't think of anything with Lara looking at me like that. So I started crying, which made everything feel even worse. Last I remember, Lara was trying to talk to me, to get me to calm down, but I couldn't bear to see that look in her eyes anymore. So I went home.

FRIDAY, JANUARY 27, 9:23 P.M.

Lara came over to see me. I almost didn't let her in because I couldn't face her, as guilty as I felt. But I'm glad I did. She didn't come to lecture me more. In fact, she even admitted that it was wrong to dump the whole thing on me.

Yes, I did one shitty thing, but she pointed out that obviously this book has been a fount of evil for centuries. And none of us is innocent—we all took part in the rituals, and we all wanted to believe that the book could be used for good, as long as it was serving our purposes. But we each brought a little dark energy into those rituals, our own ugly desires.

Lara said the important thing is to recognize it and do whatever we can to make it right. I want to believe her, but I have no idea what that might entail, or what difference it could possibly make. Can saying I'm sorry really conquer this ancient and powerful evil? Lara said she doesn't know. But we have to try. And the first step is going back to White Rabbit and apologizing to Derek.

SATURDAY, JANUARY 28, 11:03 P.M.

This "making amends" thing is going to be harder than I thought. We went back to White Rabbit today, and there was already a sign that read *Closed Indefinitely* in the window. When I saw that, I was ready to give up and go home, but Lara wouldn't be put off so easily. She peered through a chink in the papered-up windows and spotted that the lights were on and someone was inside. So she banged on the door until the owner finally came over and opened it up. And he was like, *Can you read? We're closed, we're going out of business.* But Lara insisted that we had to talk to him and after a while he sighed and let us in.

The store looked different from the last time I'd been in. It was clear that we caught Derek packing up all his wares— there were piles of books and stacks of boxes everywhere, most of them with their flaps hanging open as he carefully recorded the location of each item before sealing it away. It was horrible to think of how the agents of the church were destroying this man's life's work overnight.

Lara asked Derek about it, and he talked about how bad things have gotten so quickly. The mega-church has hassled him in one way or another for years, but he never dreamed it would end up like this—not only for him, but the whole town. He said it was almost like they were under some kind of curse.

Which isn't that far from the truth, really. Lara looked over at me when he said that, and I knew that was my cue to come clean. So I told him about the book, and how I'd stolen it that day, and now it's in the hands of the mega-church, and everything is a disaster.

I'm not sure if he believed the whole story—it is pretty outlandish, I suppose, from an outside perspective. But he shrugged and said it made as much sense as any other explanation he's heard for what's going on.

I told him I was really sorry, and that I'd do anything I could to make it up to him. Derek laughed. What could I do? Even if I could come up with the price of the book, that wasn't going to save his store now. I asked if he wanted me to go to the cops, but he pointed out that they were as corrupt as anyone now, and definitely not on his side.

What he really wanted was for everything to go back to normal.

That's a nice idea, but I don't know how the hell I can make that promise. But Lara assured him we'd do everything we could to make it happen. She said if we can figure out a way to get the book back and destroy it, we might be able to turn back what happened and make things right again. I wish I had even a little of her confidence.

WEDNESDAY, FEBRUARY 1, 6:13 P.M.

I'm starting to get really scared about what's going on. I feel like such an idiot for everything I've done to get us into this situation. But then, how was I supposed to know? Sure, I knew that slipping that book into my bag and walking out of the store wasn't the *most* admirable course of action, but how could I have ever guessed it would open some kind of portal to hell?

All those spells we did—they seemed harmless at the time. Though after a while the evidence started to mount that we were in over our heads. Why didn't I back out then?

I don't know. I've been over it a million times in my head, but I can't disentangle the threads. I know I made some bad decisions, and I was willfully blind to the consequences of my actions because I was enjoying being lucky, being popular, and feeling like I had these special talents and abilities.

Looking back on it, I also see times that I don't think I was completely in control of what was going on. The feeling I always had when I did those drawings . . . I didn't want to acknowledge it, but it seems clear now that there was some kind of demonic possession going on, like Caleb witnessed back when he was a kid. Maybe it's been there from the very first day, even when I took the book from the store—there was something guiding me then, the same force that made it impossible for me to write anything in the book until we figured out that it wanted magic spells. How much choice did I really have in all this?

I know that sounds like a cop-out, like I'm trying to deflect from my own responsibility. But in a way, I'd rather claim the responsibility. Because if I did all this—if it came from something inside me, then I can decide to end it, to fix it. But if there is some other force that's controlling my urges and my actions, how can I trust anything about myself? The very idea that the thoughts in my head might not be my own—it's terrifying. How can I possibly choose what path to take under these circumstances? Knowing all the while that what feels like good intentions could be a trap laid by this demon force?

THURSDAY, FEBRUARY 2, 8:19 P.M.

Well, we have a plan now, if not a very promising one.

Today after another surreal day at school, we all reconvened at Lucas's place to try to figure out what to do next. Lucas was arguing that we shouldn't do anything at all. In his view, we've already done more than enough damage in all our interactions with the book. It became our responsibility when it passed into our hands, but now that someone else has it, it's not our problem anymore.

I have to admit, this argument is pretty appealing. But Caleb said it was too late to do that—between the spell craft and the drawings, it's clear that the demons have already infested us, and if we sit back and let what's happening happen, we're as good as signing our souls over to the Devil.

It was alarming to hear Caleb talk this way, to be honest.

Ever since Lucas's love spell, Caleb has always been the one pushing for us to make more and better use of the Book of Shadows. But even he had to acknowledge that it had all gone too far now. I think he's really worried about what will happen to his dad—both in this world, and the next.

It's a new side of Caleb, but if whatever we did with that Book of Shadows has driven him back to his religious roots, maybe it will at least be useful to us. When it comes to the Devil and his minions, Caleb knows what he's talking about, and he says the only way to defeat magical beings is with magic. He suggested we figure out whatever spell Hecate's mom did, to bind the demons and send them back where they came from. But Lara was dead set against this idea. She pointed out that we don't actually know any magic . . . not really. She said we couldn't actually see it because none of us ever tried to do spell work before we came across the Book of Shadows, but she had. And Lara had been nervous about this whole thing since our very first spell together, because she could tell that we were tapping into something way beyond anything she'd ever managed on her own. At first she let herself believe it was because we were working in group, but pretty soon it became obvious that it was the Book of Shadows doing all the real magical work. The demonic forces possessing the book—they wanted us to succeed, or to feel like we were succeeding, so they made it happen. That was their path into our world. And without their influence, we're nothing but a bunch of kids messing around.

I think at this point, with all we've seen and done, even Caleb has to admit she is probably right. We wanted to believe that we were adepts, master magicians—but none of us has any power without the Book of Shadows. And the power of the Book of Shadows can't be trusted.

Of course, that didn't leave us with many options. So with everyone miserable and demoralized, I suggested the only path left that I could think of: dealing with this the human way, not the magical one. We talk to Caleb's dad and try to reason with him. Maybe we can get the book back and destroy it.

It's a long shot in so many ways—will Caleb's dad talk to us? Will we be able to convince him to hand over the book? And even if we get it, will destroying it do any good, or is it too late for that?

But we've run out of other options, so this is the best one we've got.

SUNDAY, FEBRUARY 5, 9:50 A.M.

I'm sitting here with the others in one of the church's unused conference rooms, typing into my phone to keep myself sane. We all know we have to do something to stop Reverend Gardner from using the Book of Shadows, but what?

I still can't believe what I've seen. If the others hadn't been there to confirm it for me . . . This isn't fun and games anymore, if it ever was. There is a force out there—something we've unleashed—that won't rest until it has infected everyone in this city. And once it gets beyond this city? God only knows where it will stop.

If I thought getting Caleb's dad to either give us the Book of Shadows or destroy it was going to be as simple as asking politely, well, that was pretty far off the mark. Caleb warned us it wouldn't be that easy, especially given their tense relationship lately, but I don't think any of us realized what we were up against.

Caleb's bright idea was to intercept his dad before services on Sunday. Since Caleb's been living at Lucas's and his father has been busy converting the entire city, it was the one time all week when we could be pretty sure we knew where he'd be. Whatever else is going on, Caleb knows that his dad always spends the hour before his Sunday service in the church office, putting the finishing touches on his sermon.

Sure enough, he was there. He even called out "come in" when Caleb knocked, and for a brief moment, I thought maybe this would all be easier than we anticipated. Reverend Gardner looked approachable enough, bent over his desk with a pen in hand as he scratched at the paper in front of him. That is, until he looked up and saw Caleb. Then his whole manner changed: his face went dark with anger, and his knuckles turned white where he was gripping his pen.

He snapped at Caleb and the rest of us to get out of his sight, but Caleb stood his ground as he tried to explain to his father the importance of our mission. But before he had even gotten around to mentioning the Book of Shadows, his father was on his feet, red faced and trembling, cursing him and the rest of us the way only a Bible-thumping minister can.

From then on, it was a tirade of "You're no son to me, I do not see you, I do not recognize you, you are dead to me." Caleb withstood it all, but I could see him flinch when his father accused him of being in league with Satan and an agent of the Devil. That was when Lara tried to intervene on his behalf, but that caused Reverend Gardner to turn on her, calling her a "corrupting influence" and a "Jezebel."

Finally Lucas tried to make him listen to reason, telling him that his soul was in danger, and explaining that the book was exerting a dark influence on him. At that, Reverend Gardner stopped and seemed at least to register his words. He hesitated a moment, and I saw his eyes slide down to his desk. That's when I realized with a cold shock that it wasn't an ordinary piece of paper or notebook he had been writing on when we entered—it was the Book of Shadows.

Reverend Gardner didn't pause long. He shook his head, insisting that he wouldn't listen to our "fork-tongued lies." Then he started ranting about how he was being rewarded after all these years for his faith and fellowship, and how the Lord had given him a holy tool by which he would build a kingdom of peace on the Earth, with himself as its master. In some ways, it was exactly the rhetoric you expect from a minister of an evangelical church, but there was something in his tone, some fire in his eyes that made his sentiments feel entirely unchristian. He might still be referencing God's glory, but it was clear that it was dreams of his own glory that were consuming him.

Against my better judgment, I took advantage of his momentary distraction and moved toward the book on his desk. Had he really been composing his sermons all this time in this book of black magic? This book that had twisted and perverted everything we'd ever written in it, to advance its own ends?

As I looked down at the page open on the desk before me, a wave of horror came over me. I would have slumped to the ground if Caleb's father hadn't noticed me at that moment and grabbed me by the arm.

The others had clearly given up hope of reclaiming the book and were already moving toward the door. I struggled to free myself from Reverend Gardner's grasp so I could join them. I tried to yell at him to let me go, but my breath caught in my throat as I looked into his face. It only lasted a second or two, but it was the same effect I had noticed in that underground chamber during our necromancy ritual. Reverend Gardner's face was melting and transforming before my eyes, taking on strange features like the creatures I've been drawing all these months.

"Stay away from that," he hissed and growled from a twisted, fanged mouth. "God gave it to me to do my holy work. I've been working on this sermon all week."

But the writing on that page—it wasn't a sermon. I could see clearly now that it was a list: a list of names. Strange names, and I only recognized a couple of them, but it was enough to know. Reverend Gardner had sat at this desk for the past week, thinking he was composing some sermon for his congregation, when actually he was painstakingly listing the names of every demon in hell.

And in ten minutes, the service will begin. And he's going to read this list to his parishioners. Who can say what havoc will be unleashed then?

SUNDAY, FEBRUARY 5, 10:13 A.M.

Still here in the conference room. Reverend Gardner left for the service, and I'm trying to write down everything we were talking about, hoping that it will help us figure out what to do next.

It seems so crazy, what has happened with the reverend, even though we all saw it with our own eyes. Lucas keeps asking, how can it be that the forces of evil are working through a man of God? But Lara and Caleb don't seem all that surprised. Caleb especially—he keeps repeating that "the Devil can quote scripture to his own ends," and that he'll take any path he can to corrupt humanity, up to and including sacred institutions like churches.

But if even churches can be corrupted, who will stop this force? I don't think there is anyone else who can, anyone else who even understands the full extent of what's going on.

Caleb again suggested using magic, and Lara launched into her objection about how all the magic we've done has come *from* this dark source, so how can we use that same magic to turn it away? But at this point . . . We tried the human approach. We tried everything we can think of. What other options are there?

Shit, something just happened! I don't know how to describe it . . . it was almost like a giant thunderclap, except instead of coming from the sky, it sounded—it *felt*—like it was coming from all around us. From the air. And now there's something that sounds like . . . voices? Only they sound unnaturally warped and inhuman. What the hell is that?

Caleb says it's coming from the church hall. The service must have started—Reverend Gardner's demonically inspired service. That can't be good.

SUNDAY, FEBRUARY 5, 4:42 P.M.

I can't believe it's come to this. If I had known when I started down this path . . . But it's too late now. God, what have we done? I can hardly believe what I experienced, even though I was there. Writing it all down is the only thing that's keeping me from completely losing my mind right now.

After that strange thundery noise/feeling we experienced in the conference room, we all followed Caleb into the main hall of the church, where the service was taking place. If you can even call it a service.

I wasn't at all prepared for the sight that greeted us there. All this time, I've always known this church was referred to as a "mega-church"—I've called it that myself. And I knew that meant it had a lot of members—way more than the Catholic church I go to sometimes with my parents. But I'd never been in it before, and I don't think I ever quite grasped how enormous the room itself is. It was massive, practically like an indoor football stadium, only instead of all the seats being laid out in an oval, focusing on a playing field in the center, they were all pointed in the same direction, toward the stage at the front. The stage struck me as surprisingly empty—there was no altar, no candles, no artwork to attract the eye. Nothing but a lectern that looked tiny compared to the massive scale of the room, and behind that lectern, one tiny looking man. Reverend Gardner.

But that wasn't where the audience's attention was directed—it would have been pointless to look down on him, since you could hardly see him at such a distance. Instead the thousands and thousands of people gathered together in the church had their faces turned up toward a series of giant screens that hung high above the stage. As Caleb's dad swayed back and forth behind that lectern, a bank of cameras were filming his every move in close up, and projecting it onto the screens above us. I glanced up, but I wasn't prepared for queasy horror of seeing his pale, quivering, sweat-slicked face displayed on countless screens, in full color and high definition.

As he swayed, he clutched a microphone in his hands so you could hear his sermon echoing weirdly throughout the auditorium. But it wasn't a sermon, not really. He was simply reading off that list of horrible names in his great, booming voice. I looked around to see how the congregation was reacting to this strange turn of events, but it was clear he had them in his thrall. They stood there, thousands of them, almost the whole city crowded together in this massive room in their colorful Sunday clothes, their heads and hands raised as if receiving a blessing. But their eyes were glazed and unfocused, and with one terrifying voice, they repeated Reverend Gardner's demonic litany.

And then, before our eyes, there was an overwhelming buzzing of energy in the room. At first I assumed that it must be something supernatural, but after a second I realized it was the lighting that had changed. When we entered, the auditorium was mostly darkened to draw as much attention as possible to the brightly lit stage down front. But the lights had changed—the glaring bright white of the stage lights had been replaced with deep blues and reds that swept around the room, flickering wildly like a display at a rock concert. I could imagine how, during an ordinary church service, this might be exciting and even inspiring, but under the circumstances it felt strangely sinister—especially as the red spotlights chased one another over Reverend Gardner's face, still projected hugely over the hall.

That was when it happened. As I stared up at the giant displays with their multiplied, identical images, Reverend Gardner's face began to shift and bubble on the screens, in rhythm to the chanting of the congregation. The colors deepened and bled, and the lines and shapes warped into something completely different—things I soon recognized as the creatures from my drawings, only ten times more hideous now that they were gigantic and in full color. At first I couldn't tell if it was a trick of my eyes, but it seemed like the demons were struggling out of the boxes of the screens, desperately shoving their way into our world, and gaining power every second—as if Hecate's prediction of the demons' ultimate goal was coming true right in front of us.

I felt Lucas grasp my arm and tug. "This is messed up," he whispered. "We have to get out of here." I was all in favor of this plan and ready to leave, but Lara stopped us and made us stay.

She said, "We can't leave now, or this will only get worse. We have to get the book and destroy it."

I wanted to ask her how the hell she planned to do that, but Caleb didn't wait around for further discussion. As soon as the words left her mouth, he started sprinting down the center aisle toward the stage where his father stood. I half expected any of the zillion people in the audience to jump out and stop him, but they were all too fully immersed in their trance—none even seemed to take any notice of him. We all stood frozen for a minute as Caleb reached the stage and hauled himself up on it. He grabbed his father and shoved him away from the lectern. There was a strange noise as the air went out of Reverend Gardner, and his amplified voice fell suddenly silent. But that didn't stop the congregation, who somehow kept up their endless chanting of those hideous names.

From where I stood, I could see Caleb trying to wrestle his father away from the lectern, and working desperately to help him shake off the demonic influence. He even slapped him a couple of times, in hopes of breaking the trance, but it was no use.

As Caleb and his father struggled for control of the lectern, Lucas dashed forward to protect his friend. He hurtled down the aisle, and Lara quickly rushed after him. Lucas got there first and took advantage of Reverend Gardner's distraction and seized the book. He pulled a lighter from his pocket and held it to one corner of the book. The flame rose up for a moment, then fizzled, releasing an ugly smell. Lucas tried again, holding the lighter to the corner for longer this time.

I held my breath, but after a minute or so the fire seemed to take. The small flame developed into a larger, crackling blaze, and I could feel its heat from where I stood. Then suddenly it was as if the fire had run into some bizarre chemical vein. With a hideous howling noise, the flames shot up into the air until there was a column of fire pouring forth from the book. As we watched, it shifted in color. First deep orange and scarlet, then blinding white, then bluish green, and finally an unnatural and terrifying black, as if it was no longer fire but its opposite, the flames like dancing shadows. The harsh scent of sulfur filled the air, and the column of fire turned to a cloud of thick smoke and ash. When the cloud settled the book was still there, looking the same as ever.

"Tear it," I yelled to him. I had been able to cut out a page from the book months ago, maybe that would work again. Lucas seemed too dazed to follow my instruction, so I ran up and pulled myself onto the stage. I approached the lectern and focused on the book laying flat on its surface, trying not to think about the intimidatingly huge mob in front of me, still stand-ing enthralled. I opened the book up to a random page in the middle—one of my drawings—and started to tear the page from the binding. It held fast at first, but with some effort I heard a ripping sound and it started to come away in my hand. I felt a momentary sense of triumph and started in on another page.

That's when the blood started to well up.

Pretty soon there was blood everywhere, and I could feel a strange vibration in the air around me, like a voiceless scream. I had a sense of satisfaction at first that I was causing harm to this evil thing, but as the blood spread, I began to notice some-thing: the puddles on the stage were coagulating and scabbing up. I stepped away with shaking hands as I realized that it was reforming itself into flat sheets, which slid across the surface of the stage, sealed themselves into the binding of the book, and grew pale, turning into pages of writing and drawing once again. I realized that it was no use: nothing we did physically would ever damage or destroy the book. The magic in it was simply too strong.

With hands and clothes still spattered with this unholy blood, I started to back away, desperate to get as far as possible from the situation. But Lara caught me and held me fast. She was saying something, but it took a while for me to make sense of it over the chanting of the congregation and my own rising terror. At last I realized that it was an incantation—the very first incantation we ever did together, in an attempt to cleanse the book of negative energy.

"Spirits of nature, cleanse this object of negative energies and bring blessings of light upon it."

I couldn't believe what I was hearing. We'd already agreed that there was no way we had magic powerful enough to defeat this possessed object. And that spell in particular, it was such a simple little thing, and obviously it had already failed to work once. But I remembered what Lara had said in the White Rabbit bookstore, about how the spell couldn't work since I, as owner of the book, was participating in bad faith by not accepting my own role in bringing dark energy to the book. Maybe I could fix that this time, if I was sincere in my contrition for what I've done. This time, I definitely was.

I took Lara's hand and began repeating her words as forcefully as I could, visualizing positive energy to counteract the horrors around me. Eventually I noticed that Lucas took her other hand and joined us. Caleb, meanwhile, was still struggling with his father, who continued to recite demon names.

Even though Reverend Gardner was no longer amplified, it hardly mattered with the whole of the congregation still reciting them too. With all those thousands and thousands of voices, it seemed impossible for our little charm to outweigh them. Still, we kept on.

And to my surprise, something did happen—the more we chanted, the more I could feel the shift of power in the room. There was something oddly familiar about it now—it was like the pulsing energy I had felt every time we'd gotten together to perform one of our rituals. But at the same time, there was something different about it. I was used to feeling powerful vibrations surging through my body, but this time it was as though there were two types of vibrations, on different wavelengths. It was like the very air around us was warping. And feeling them both at the same time was both thrilling and painful, almost like being ripped in two. But the pain wasn't in my physical body. It's hard to describe but if I had to locate it anywhere, I'd say it was in my soul.

Then a new voice joined us. It was Caleb, and he had managed to free himself from his father's grip and work his way to the microphone. At first, he recited the Wiccan incantation along with us, but after a few rounds of that he switched to something else . . . something I didn't recognize at first. It took me a while to realize that he wasn't reciting anymore. He was preaching.

I couldn't catch all of what he was saying, but I remember phrases here and there: "And they shall no more offer their sacrifices to Devils, after whom they have gone a whoring;" "That ancient serpent, who is called the Devil and Satan, the deceiver of the whole world;" "And the dragon stood before the woman who was about to give birth, so that when she bore her child he might devour it." It was creepy, and almost as intense as whatever the congregation was chanting. But it seemed to work, in some way. The amplification of the speakers carried his voice to the farthest corners of the theater. I noticed Lara and Lucas had abandoned their chanting to listen to Caleb, and I stopped too. It was breathtaking—that smooth yet insistent voice, effortlessly claiming command of the room. More than ever before, I saw what his father had seen in him—all the potential to be a great charismatic leader. But I could see what had scared Caleb about that too. So much power, and so easy to abuse. Just like his father abused it, even before he got his hands on the book. Maybe too much power for any one human.

Looking around, I realized that we weren't the only people who had stopped chanting. The rest of the congregation had stopped too. It was like they had been broken free of their trance, and were staring around in confusion, as if awaking from a strange dream. Many of them were looking up at the thirty-foot screens, which no longer showed the strange demonic figures from my drawings, but were now focused on Caleb's face, calmly and steadily preaching his impromptu sermon. Even Caleb's father stood off to the side, staring at him transfixed.

"It's working," I said to the others. "Keep going, Caleb. It's working!"

But as I glanced over at Lara, I saw a look of horror fixed on her face as she watched Caleb preach. I followed her eyes and that's when I saw it: where a second ago, Caleb's face had seemed calm and placid, I now saw that it was screwed up in concentration and physical effort. And more than that—it wasn't only his expression that was twisted, but his features themselves, bulging and seething into strange and terrible formations. His lips spread over hideous fangs, which then turned into a thick black beak, only to transform again into a gaping toothless maw. His eyes, too, grew big like a frog's and then tiny and black like a bird's. It was like no creature I've ever seen on Earth.

Somehow, Caleb's intervention had made him the new target of the demons, and they were devouring him body and soul. It was too awful, seeing him so distorted, and I looked away—only to have my eyes alight on the inescapable screens all around the space, projecting his terrifying transformation in images thirty feet high.

Lara at last distracted me from this nightmarish vision by pulling her hand from my grip. Freed from her paralysis, she rushed forward and grabbed Caleb around the chest, tugging him away from the lectern while screaming at him to stop. I moved to help her, hoping against hope that it wasn't too late to save Caleb and return him to his normal form. But he resisted us, breaking his speech for only a moment as he fought us off. Then he was again declaiming into the microphone, clearly determined to draw all the demonic attacks toward himself and away from us, from the congregation, from his father.

Meanwhile the magical energy and tension in the room was rising and rising, far beyond anything we had achieved during our private rituals. Then came a thunderous *crack* that seemed to release it all. I looked behind me and saw one of the great central pillars in the middle of the auditorium had splintered and was beginning to collapse. Before I could even process what was happening, there was another crack and a second pillar started to sag under the weight of the lofty roof. A cloud of dust and debris formed and began to settle down on the crowd below.

Another crack, and one of the Jumbotrons came crashing to the ground in a shower of sparks, which ignited some scaffolding behind the main stage. Then huge billows of dark smoke joined the cloud of debris, and the pungent smell of burning materials filled the air. Pandemonium took hold as the congregants finally recognized what was happening and began to stream for the exits, but still I stood frozen.

At last Lucas broke me free of the spell by yelling my name and urging me to get out of the church before it fell completely to pieces around us. I grabbed Lara's hand again and dragged her with me through the growing wreckage. I could hardly see more than a foot in front of me at this point, and Caleb's voice was becoming increasingly distorted by the malfunctioning sound system. Somehow, we made it out to the parking lot minutes before the entire structure came crashing down.

I looked around and found Lucas only a few feet away from us. I felt a surge of relief, followed by an undertow of dread as I realized what it meant that he was standing alone. Lucas seemed to read the question on my face. "I tried," he said. "I tried to get him to come with me. He told me to take his father, make sure he made it out safely, so I did. I thought Caleb was right behind me, but . . ." Lucas trailed off meaningfully as we both looked over at the smoldering wreckage that had once been the mega-church. Caleb's voice no longer emanated from the speakers—the only sound was the crackling of fire and the steadily increasing wail of sirens coming to deal with the unexpected destruction.

WEDNESDAY, MARCH 15, 4:32 P.M.

The last few weeks have been really rough. Ever since Caleb's funeral, I haven't been able to manage more than going through the motions of existing. I couldn't bring myself to write here. For a while I was too overwhelmed by the sadness of the events. Caleb, for all the challenging aspects of his personality, was well-known and well-loved in this community, and the days and weeks following his death sometimes seemed like an endless parade of memorials and dedications of one form or another. It's so strange not having him around.

The worst thing is not knowing exactly what happened back in that church. It kills me that I don't even know what Caleb's last moments were like. Whatever happened, though, I don't believe he died in vain. Because something definitely changed after that day. We lost Caleb, but we are starting to get our city back.

The biggest change is that the reign of the mega-church is over. I don't think anyone in the general public quite knows or is willing to acknowledge exactly what happened in there that day. The most common story is that the church had been shoddily constructed from the beginning, that it had been expanded again and again without regard to local building codes, and that it was a disaster waiting to happen. Certain insiders now say that the structural flaws in the building had been a known problem for years. Even more damning, the money from a major fund-raising campaign to fix them had disappeared—apparently into the pockets of some highly placed church administrators.

That bit of gossip has led some to whisper darkly that the whole enterprise was cursed all along. That Reverend Gardner had always been corrupt and power mad, and that this tragedy was a divine comeuppance.

Of course, some stalwarts describe the whole event as a miracle, because of all the thousands of people crammed into that building, in the end, only thirty-six were killed by the destruction. Thirty-six people, including Caleb. It's hard for me to see that in a very positive light.

Among the survivors are a group of people who tried to start up a collection to rebuild the church. They talked a good game about how they were going to build it even bigger and mightier than before, to show the power of God's love or whatever. They didn't get very far, though. Caleb's dad had always been the driving force behind the mega-church, and it seems like he's finally getting out of that racket.

That's right: Reverend Gardner has retired from the church business, leaving the whole congregation at loose ends. You can hardly blame him, having witnessed his only son's death like that. I wonder sometimes what he knows, what he understands of what really happened in that church. He of all people should get it—he's spent years raging against the Devil in all his forms and was well-versed in matters of the occult, so you'd think he'd recognize those forces in his own church, attacking his own son.

Plus, unlike most people, Caleb's dad knew about the Book of Shadows and was one of the few outside our circle to grasp its power. After all, he himself had obviously fallen victim to its temptations in the days before the fire. I can only imagine that he feels guilty and somewhat personally responsible for what happened to Caleb. But he isn't talking about it—not publicly, anyway. His only statement has been something vague about tragedies both personal and communal, and that he feels he has "lost his calling."

I wonder what anyone in that massive congregation thinks of or remembers about what happened in the church. There have been a handful of people who were present, and who have come forward to say they saw or felt the Devil that day, but I don't think anyone has taken them very seriously. They're either regarded as crazed zealots, or else it's assumed they're speaking metaphorically. As for the rest—thousands of people—everyone seems to have settled on the same version of events: Caleb's father was preaching his normal Sunday sermon when his estranged son burst in and started some kind of argument. In the chaos that followed, the structure of the church began to fall apart. No one is exactly sure what touched it off at that particular moment, though some people have hypothesized that some electrical fire was sparked by one of the speakers or screens.

In the meantime other local churches whose attendance had

dwindled since the mega-church came to town have opened their doors to the displaced, and religious life in the city has started to redistribute more evenly. The mega-church even sold the newspaper and TV station back to their original owners in an effort to raise money to settle certain lawsuits that arose in the aftermath of the destruction.

So in that sense at least, things are getting back to normal. In fact, things are going back to a "normal" I've never even known—the way things were before the mega-church came to town and twisted everything, taking over the life of the city. The way things were before I was even born. Now it's nothing but a normal town with normal religious activity, and not one super powerful church controlling everything. It's good, but it's also really strange to me and my friends, and the other kids my age who have never known a world that wasn't totally dominated by church rhetoric. People at school have become much less God-obsessed, and have been getting into a lot of other activities. It's a mixed blessing, as drunk driving incidents and teen pregnancies have gone up, but at the same time there's a lot more tolerance and good feeling all around, instead of the church's rigid Puritanism dominating everyone's behavior.

There was one last piece of business Lara, Lucas, and I needed to attend to before we could move forward with our lives. Lucas texted us both the day after the event to ask what we thought had happened to the Book of Shadows. Lara and I were both sure it must have been finally destroyed along with everything else in the church, but Lucas wasn't so sure, and suggested we at least go check it out before the whole site was cleared out by bulldozers and treasure hunters.

Lucas was right. We went over in the middle of the night

to avoid work crews and other curious onlookers, and under cover of darkness dug around a bit in the wreckage where the stage and lectern once stood. And there we found it—totally unharmed, despite the massive destruction all around. Not so much as a ripped page or a singe mark on the cover. That's how strong the evil in this object was. I realized then, this must be why Rosemary used that potion to clear off the pages. It wasn't because she couldn't bring herself to destroy it completely—she must have tried to destroy it and discovered that its magic was too strong. The ritual she used on the book was her last-ditch attempt to contain its evil.

I held the book in trembling hands as we all looked at one another helplessly. It was only too clear at that point that we lacked the magical power necessary to have any chance of defeating or destroying the book. At last Lucas made the only reasonable suggestion: if we couldn't destroy it, we could at least hide it. All the trouble we encountered and caused came because of our physical interactions with the book: writing in it, drawing in it, reading and enacting the rituals it suggested. If no human had physical access to it, maybe at least those things could be avoided.

After some deliberation, we settled on a spot where it should stay hidden for a good long time. I have no confidence that this is the end of the book's history—now that I know its incredible power, I can't really bring myself to believe that it is gone for good. But I hope we've at least sent it into hibernation for a while, and with any luck, it will be many generations before it turns up again. When and if it is ever found, I can only hope it will be by someone with more experience and self-control than we had.

There is some reason for optimism, at least. Since we got rid of the book, a lot of its magic seems to weakened. The spells we wrought together seem to have been mostly broken. I don't think any of us feels very lucky anymore, my popularity has faded away, and Tyler and Lucas's relationship is over too. That might be partly because Lucas finally came clean and told Tyler about the love spell. The three of us had agreed not to tell anyone about the Book of Shadows, for fear that they might seek it out themselves and reawaken its now dormant powers. But Lucas decided to make an exception for Tyler—he thought it was only fair that Tyler should have the full story of what happened to him.

Even knowing the truth, I don't know if Tyler will ever completely recover from what we did. Last I heard, he was in intensive therapy, trying to figure out who he really is without the influence of our spells or the mega-church's preaching. I hope it works.

One last thing was bothering me, though: I let those demonically inspired drawings of mine get copied and passed around in the literary journal. I have no idea if they have the same conjuring power outside of the book as they did within it, but I always got an awful feeling when I saw them around.

To settle my own fears, I've gone around gathering up every copy of the school lit journal they were printed in that I can find. Then I burned them all in a bonfire with Lucas and Lara while we recited a protective incantation. A little part of me was sad to see the last records of all my drawings be destroyed, but I know it's for the best. I understand now that those drawings never really came from me, and it was only pride and self-delusion that convinced me they did. They were never anything more than a tool for evil to find its foothold in this world, and I won't have that on my conscience any longer. I only hope our little ritual took—at least these copies did actually burn.

So that ends our role in this centuries-old drama of good versus evil. May it be a long time before the next chapter is written.

Rest in peace, Caleb. And thank you for your sacrifice.

E-MAIL TRANSCRIPT

From: Melanie V.
To: Montague Verano
Date: Monday, August 21, at 10:20 P.M.
Subject: Book of Shadows

Dear Professor Verano,

You don't know me, but I hope you will read this message and take it seriously. I don't know where else to turn. I found your previous books in the library today while hunting for some way to deal with what's going on, and I hoped that you might be sympathetic to my situation. Maybe with all your expertise on the occult, you might even be able to see a way out of this mess. My only hope is that you'll be able to help me before more people are killed, or worse.

My friends and I got ourselves into some deep trouble with a magical object. We tried everything we could think of to fix it ourselves, and in the end we figured our best bet was to hide it where no one would ever find it and use it again. That seemed to work for a while, but lately I think the Book of Shadows's curse is following us even from its hiding place.

The only people who knew the whole truth about the Book of Shadows were me and my friends Lara, Lucas, and Caleb. Caleb was killed earlier this year fighting off the demonic entities infesting the book—that was before we hid it. After that we thought the nightmare was over, but Lara was killed a few months later in a car accident. And yesterday I learned that Lucas was found dead of an apparent suicide during his first week of college.

This could all be coincidence, but I'm scared that I will be next. And if I die now, no one will know the full story of the Book of Shadows, and whoever finds it next might unknowingly unleash its evil again.

I kept a diary during the whole period when we experimented with the Book of Shadows, and I'm enclosing it along with this e-mail, so at least one other person will have the full story. In it is everything I know about the history and power and danger of this object. I hope you will know better what to do with this information than we ever did.

Melanie Vong

[address and phone number redacted]

EDITOR'S NOTE

I spoke on the phone to the young woman referred to in these pages as "Melanie" shortly after receiving this missive. Thanks to my stature in the field of parapsychology and the supernatural, of course I've received any number of inquiries of this nature in the past few years, and on further investigation many turn out to be pranks or hoaxes.

A story this extraordinary demands extraordinary evidence, and I asked Melanie what corroboration she could provide for the events she described in her diary. Melanie offered me a small collection of cell-phone photos, along with a few newspaper articles confirming the destruction of the church described at the end of this narrative, but it was not enough to provide conclusive evidence of occult phenomena.

I then explained to Melanie that the story would be almost

EDITOR'S NOTE

I spoke on the phone to the young woman referred to in these pages as "Melanie" shortly after receiving this missive. Thanks to my stature in the field of parapsychology and the supernatural, of course I've received any number of inquiries of this nature in the past few years, and on further investigation many turn out to be pranks or hoaxes.

A story this extraordinary demands extraordinary evidence, and I asked Melanie what corroboration she could provide for the events she described in her diary. Melanie offered me a small collection of cell-phone photos, along with a few newspaper articles confirming the destruction of the church described at the end of this narrative, but it was not enough to provide conclusive evidence of occult phenomena.

I then explained to Melanie that the story would be almost

impossible to confirm without access to the object itself—the so-called "Book of Shadows." Melanie was wisely hesitant at first to give me any information about the location of the cursed object, but I reassured her of my experience in such matters, and that she could trust me to handle the information safely and appropriately. Though still reluctant, Melanie eventually gave me the necessary coordinates to help me locate the book.

It was about a week after that conversation that I was saddened to learn of Melanie's death, resulting from a freak electrical accident.

As is obvious from these pages, Melanie was a brave, independent, and intelligent young woman who made some dangerous errors in judgment. But when she saw the error of her ways, she made every possible effort to atone for her mistakes and protect others from suffering their consequences. For this, I admire her.

I feel certain that to save others from making the same mistakes she made, Melanie would have wanted her story to reach as many people as possible. For this reason, I took particular pains to seek out the Book of Shadows she and her friends so carefully hid, as this narrative could hardly be successful without that document.

Even knowing the coordinates, this was no easy feat. Melanie and her friends had chosen to rid themselves of the object by weighing it down with heavy stones and dumping it at the bottom of an artificial lake made from a local rock quarry. The lake was deep and difficult to navigate, and it took many months, a great deal of specialized gear, and a team of trained aquatic archeologists, as well as a few committed student volunteers to discover the book under the shifting sands at the bottom—all which, it must be said, was made possible by a generous grant from the Institute for Paranormal and Supernatural Investigation (better known as IPSI).

From there, I oversaw a painstaking restoration process to salvage the drawings made by Mel and return them to their original appearance.

I recognize that toward the end of this narrative, Melanie grew concerned that even reproductions of her demonically inspired drawings might have a negative effect on those who saw them, which is why she went to the trouble of gathering up and destroying the photocopied editions of her school's literary magazine. I, however, consider this extremely unlikely, which is why I have chosen to include Melanie's illustrations in this version of the text. Rest assured, the originals remain safe in my own library.

Montague Verano, PhD
Independent Investigator of Paranormal Phenomena
Moscow, Idaho